1776—And All That

ALSO BY LEONARD WIBBERLEY

Mrs. Searwood's Secret Weapon
Stranger at Killnock
The Quest of Excalibur
Take Me to Your President
McGillicuddy McGotham
Beware of the Mouse
The Mouse That Roared
The Mouse on the Moon
The Mouse on Wall Street
A Feast of Freedom
The Island of the Angels
The Hands of Cormac Joyce
The Road from Toomi
Adventures of an Elephant Boy
The Centurion
Meeting with a Great Beast
The Testament of Theophilus
The Last Stand of Father Felix

NONFICTION

The Shannon Sailors
Voyage by Bus
Ah Julian!
Yesterday's Land
Towards a Distant Land
No Garlic in the Soup
The Land That Isn't There

JUVENILES (FICTION)

Deadmen's Cave
Kevin O'Connor and the Light Brigade
The Wound of Peter Wayne
John Treegate's Musket
Peter Treegate's War
Sea Captain from Salem
Treegate's Raiders
Leopard's Prey
Flint's Island
The Red Pawns

JUVENILES (NONFICTION)

Wes Powell—Conqueror of the Colorado
The Life of Winston Churchill
John Barry—Father of the Navy
The Epics of Everest
Man of Liberty—the Life of Thomas Jefferson
Young Man from the Piedmont
A Dawn in the Trees
The Gales of Spring
Time of the Harvest

1776

—And All That

(Being a true and detailed account of a
CELESTIAL VISITATION to the WHITE HOUSE
in connection with the Bicentenary of
the UNITED STATES OF AMERICA, 1776–1976)

by Leonard Wibberley

William Morrow and Company, Inc.
New York   1975

82944

1 2 3 4 5 79 78 77 76 75

Library of Congress Cataloging in Publication Data

Wibberley, Leonard Patrick O'Connor (date)
   1776—and all that.
   I. Title.
PZ4.W632Sg   [PS3573.I2]   813'.5'4   75-20061
ISBN 0-688-02969-8

"*In the United States, as everybody knows, the central representative assembly is altogether subordinate. The Senate is far more powerful and far more respected. The President is high above both. He has monarchic powers superior to anything of the kind in Europe—superior by far to those exercised by the King of Prussia in the days when that individual was also military head of the Reich.*"

—Hilaire Belloc
The Cruise of the Nona
Houghton Mifflin Co., 1925

1776—And All That

Chapter One

The archangel Gabriel was speeding down through the light years, past galaxy after galaxy, past black holes and pulsars and quasars and spiral nebulas and blue giants and red dwarfs and all the jeweled display of Space. He had been sent on an errand to Earth.

All about him, through the infinity of Space, everything from the vastest of the supergalaxies to the tiniest atomic particle scrupulously obeyed The Law. On Earth that was not the case—particularly in Washington, D.C., to which the archangel was bound. Earth was known through Space as The Place of Disobedience, and Washington, D.C., as its capital. It was a place to make even an archangel nervous, and Gabriel, hurtling through all the dimensions of the Time-Space continuum, was deeply disturbed.

It appeared to him that despite all that had been done for it, Earth might be lost to Lucifer after all. Worse, Earth might start to infect Heaven with its disobedience and thus have to be destroyed. If so, would the Creator after an eon or two start his great experiment in free choice between Good and Evil over again and in another place? Another Garden of Eden? Another two creatures released from their innocence and subjected to the test of the Tree of Knowledge?

"God forbid," said Gabriel, unwittingly shaking with his

prayer several billion light years of Space. But he quickly added, "Nonetheless, His will be done," and everything was immediately restored to normal.

On Earth, unaware of Gabriel's approach, the Social Secretary at the White House was holding one of the few press conferences in Washington in recent years which was not likely to land someone immediately in serious trouble.

"We are about to celebrate the two hundredth anniversary of the birth of our country," she told the assembled representatives of the media, "and a great deal of thought has been given by the President to what should be done, here in Washington and at the White House, to mark this event." This wasn't an earthshaking announcement, but for a Washington press conference in the post-Truman days it wasn't bad either.

Furthermore the Social Secretary was a pert and pretty blonde from Burlington, Vermont, who had a degree in law and a nice, frank, open manner which was of far more use to her. She looked good on television, she sounded good on radio, and the society reporters who attended her conference saw in her the woman of the seventies, liberated, intelligent, and charming, and called her Jennie. Her name was actually Sarah Truesdale.

"The President has decided that the celebration should be marked at the Executive Mansion by a gala costume ball to be given on the evening of the third of July and to be culminated at midnight when he will read, over nationwide radio and television, the Declaration of Independence as passed by the Congress . . ."

"Who will be invited?" someone asked.

"The diplomatic corps, of course. Heads of states with whom we maintain relations, members of the Congress and their wives—and a number of ordinary people, selected at random."

"What do you mean at random—just names picked out of a telephone directory?"

"Each state will be asked, through its governor, to send two citizens who are not politically or economically important —just taxpayers, to be present," Jennie said. "It will be a huge affair. It will have to be staged outdoors as well as indoors. The President hopes that it will produce a sense of joy and unity in the country; a sense of oneness; of Americans really being a family whatever their differences."

"What about security?" asked someone.

"It will be a problem, but I am sure that the Secret Service, and others responsible, will be able to take care of it. All guests, of course, will be issued special credentials, and there will be many security personnel among them."

"When you say in costume, do you mean everybody has to dress up in eighteenth-century style?"

"They don't have to," said Jennie. "But the President hopes that they will. He himself will be in costume as well as his wife."

There were no awkward questions and when the press conference was over, Jennie felt pleased. It was nice to be able to hold a press conference without feeling that it was but the first move in grand jury proceedings. When the last of the TV cameramen had gone, she sat down at her desk to run over the tapes which she herself had made; and while she was doing this there was a slight tap at the door, which was opened by a tall, dignified man, a little gray about the sideburns, with a patient and understanding air. He was dressed in what Jennie realized from looking at films made by the BBC was an English hall-porter's uniform, and on the breast of his uniform he wore a number of campaign ribbons.

"I've come for the clock, miss," he said in a voice beautifully modulated and quite soothing to listen to.

"What clock?" said Jennie.

13

"That one there, miss," said the porter pointing to a beautiful grandfather clock which stood in a dark corner of the room, as if trying to hide itself in the shadows.

"That clock?" said Jennie. "But it hasn't worked for years. It's just a case."

"The Maker wants to have a look at it," said the porter. "It'll be something to do with the celebration," he added. He looked at it admiringly. "Nice, isn't it, miss? They don't make them like that anymore. All handwork. Took a lot of patience. That's what He likes best."

"Who?" asked Jennie.

"The Maker, miss. The Maker. Pity if we bumped it getting it through the door. I wonder if you could help me get it through that big window to the terrace outside?"

"Why don't we call someone to give you a hand?" asked Jennie.

"I was supposed to do it myself, miss," said the porter humbly, and Jennie looked at him and at the campaign ribbons and reflected that he was probably a veteran of some war who had been given this job in return for his services and was holding on to it rather desperately. He must have been quite handsome when he was young, and all those campaign ribbons meant that he had been daring too. A pity to be reduced to this kind of work—and afraid of losing the job.

"Okay," she said, "I'll help you." So she opened the big window, which was divided down the middle and hinged on the sides like a door. Between the two of them they got the clock outside.

"I can manage it myself from here, miss. Thank you very much," said the porter.

"Just a minute," said Jennie. "You'd better say who you are and where you are taking it to and sign for it."

"Ah, yes, miss," said the porter. "You've a good head on your shoulders if you don't mind my saying so. That might

14

be needed." She gave him a little block of paper and a pen, and he wrote something on it and handed it back to her.

"You write beautifully," she said, glancing at it.

The signature was "A. A. Gabriel."

"Nice of you to say so, miss," said the porter. "I was on Recording duty for a while," he added by way of explanation. "Well, God be with you, miss. We'll have the clock back soon, so don't fret about it."

"What a nice way to say good-bye," said Jennie.

"That's what good-bye means, miss," said the porter.

Jennie reentered her office thoughtfully and when a moment later she looked out again at the terrace, the porter had gone and the clock as well. She started up the tape of the press conference again and was listening to it with approval when there was another knock at the door and this time a young man, bursting out of a scrupulously tailored suit and with the build of a football player, entered. She had seen him about the White House before, though mostly in company with the Marine Guard, and recognized him vaguely. He was carrying a clipboard.

"Czeuleger, miss," he said. "Lieutenant Tom Czeuleger. Marine Corps."

"Oh," said Jennie. His face was impressive. It looked like that of Henry Wilcoxon, who was one of her favorites on the Late Late Show. His shoulders were broad and his presence polite but authoritative.

He reached into his pocket and produced a card and a badge which corroborated his statement, and when she had handed it back to him he said, "Might I see your identity too, please, miss?"

"Whatever for?" asked Jennie. "Everybody around here knows me."

"Routine procedure, miss," said Tom, and Jennie fumbled in her bag and produced her own badge and identification

15

card. He looked it over carefully, glancing at her every now and again. He checked her hair, her eyes, her height against the details on her card, and handed it back to her.

"Thank you, Miss Truesdale," he said. "I'm newly assigned to the Secret Service. I'm sorry to disturb you. There's to be a Presidential Ball given on the night of the third–fourth of July."

"I know," said Jennie a little snippily. "I have just finished giving a press conference announcing that."

"Yes, miss," said the lieutenant. "My men just passed the reporters out. As part of security we want to stabilize the whole White House as of today."

"Seems quite steady to me—all things considered," said Jennie.

"By stabilize," said Tom, "I mean that we are making an inventory in detail of every piece of furniture in the White House as of today. Many pieces will, in preparation for the ball, be sent out and returned. We want to know what's going out and what is returned and what was its condition before and after."

"But isn't that done all the time?" asked Jennie. "Isn't there a whole procedure already established for examining everything that is sent to the White House?"

"Everything that's sent to the *President*," said Tom. "But people have gotten lax and brought in pieces of their own so there's stuff coming in and out all the time with only a casual check on it. On the night of the ball not only will the President be here but the Vice-President—in fact the whole government of the United States, plus the heads of many countries. We just can't overlook any security details, miss."

"Are you thinking of bombs and so on?" asked Jennie.

"Just stabilizing, miss," said Tom. "When the Corps stabilizes something, it's stable. If you don't mind I'll start by

16

making an inventory of everything in the office here. But first of all is there anything missing from the office that will be returned?"

"There's an old grandfather clock. A man just came and took it away."

"A grandfather clock?" said Tom. "Does it belong to this office?"

"Actually it doesn't," said Jennie. "It belongs to the Presidential suite. It's a very old clock and it didn't work, and I suppose it was in the way and they put it down here."

"Did you identify the person who called for it?" asked Tom.

"Of course. I made him sign a receipt for it." She handed him the receipt, and he examined it carefully.

"Did you look at this when he gave it to you?" asked Tom.

"No," said Jennie. "Is there something wrong with it?"

"Well, it says that the clock is to be taken to the Maker, and the address given is 3333 Circle Drive. It's signed A. A. Gabriel."

"What's wrong with that?" asked Jennie.

"Well, if it's a very old clock you'd think the maker would be dead by now."

"He probably meant the company that made it," said Jennie. "Clockmakers stay in business for years—centuries."

"Can you describe the man who took the clock away?"

"Tall, elderly, gray at the temples, wearing some kind of porter's uniform—dark pants and a pinstriped waistcoat. He was a veteran. He wore campaign ribbons."

"Any tattoos?" asked Tom. Jennie hesitated. Had she imagined on one arm a red heart with around it in blue letters the words, "God is Love"?

"I'm not sure," she said. "I think he had a tattoo," and she described it.

17

"Probably Army," said Tom. "The Army's all hearts and flowers and so on. Well, I'll just make an inventory of what's here, miss, and I hope I won't be disturbing you."

By the time he was done, however, he had managed to arrange a date with her to go to dinner at a little restaurant in Georgetown where he said they served the best Bombay duck outside of Ho Li Wun's in Hong Kong. He was, after all, a Marine.

Chapter Two

An air of calm and of sweetest peace prevailed in Heaven as usual, and everybody was agreed that the Elysian fields had never looked so lovely. They extended for acres and acres; indeed mile on mile, sown with those lilies of the field which on Earth are called iris. There was a whole ocean of them, all in bloom, deep purple, light blue, golden yellow, the palest of pink, and white so chaste and so pure as to make the celestial clouds envious.

Here and there were deep cool groves of stately ash and graceful willow and patriarchal oaks through which the deer moved about as quiet as thought, lambs and lions took naps together, and wyverns, unicorns, and other creatures took their ease.

The unicorns liked to lie with their heads in the laps of angels, and the wyverns had a habit of snoozing in patches of sunlight where their wings glittered with a myriad of colors like stained-glass windows. Now and again one of them would wake and leap skyward and, in an excess of devotion, cry, "Gloria in excelsis Deo," and return to his sunlit couch even happier than he had been a moment before.

Voltaire, taking his morning stroll through the Fields, nodding to an astounded cardinal or priest whom he met on the way, felt happy and content. The air was warm, the flowers entrancing, and there was a murmur of bees and a fluting of birdsong all about. He nodded amiably to Saint Oliver Cromwell busy distributing Biblical tracts from the King James Version to a group of smiling and courteous Irish Catholic children, and paused to admire Saint Francis of Assisi almost lost in a crowd of adoring rabbits, lions, lambs, tigers, poodles, and crocodiles, trying to pat them all in an outpouring of love for everything God had created.

Before him, at no great distance lay The Club. It was a graceful white building in the Athenian temple style with Corinthian columns before it and large French windows opening out onto a terrace. It lay in gardens of its own, landscaped in the eighteenth-century manner—a reflecting lake here with a weeping willow mirrored in it and at the far end a small Japanese half-moon bridge; a maze to one side, and a number of flower beds all of geometrical shapes with stone-flagged walks between.

The Club was restricted to men though the way things were going, the members were not sure how long this would last. It was a place for conversation or for silence, for good heavy meals followed by good heavy sleeps, for big fireplaces in which log fires flamed and cracked on wintry days (the climate of Heaven being adjustable according to one's wishes at the moment) for sipping a glass of port or a dish of tea, for a game of bridge or a chat about politics, philosophy, and sports.

The floors were beautifully carpeted in the best Turkish style, the furniture substantial and comfortable. Voltaire decided to drop in at this excellent establishment on the chance of meeting some entertaining guest with whom to spend an hour or two in gossip. Arriving at the front door, he gave his hat and his ebony staff with the ivory knob at the top of it to the Club porter who, to Voltaire's amusement was never seen without his campaign ribbons on the breast of his uniform.

20

"Nice day, sir," said the porter, taking the hat and staff and putting them in the cloakroom.

"Enchanting," Voltaire replied. "However, enough is enough. Shut the door, *mon brave*. I feel at times that too much of the bucolic destroys a man's brains. One needs a little smoke and sulphur as a corrective."

The phrase dismayed the porter, but he said hopefully, "Nice fire in the reading room, sir. Might be what you're looking for. Air's a trifle nippy. Just right for a fire."

"Thank you," said Voltaire and entered the reading room. He found, inside, stooped over the fire and lighting a spill for a churchwarden pipe, a short, blocky man whose enormous rump was a formidable sight. The man straightened up as he entered, turned, glanced at him with a touch of suspicion, and started to puff vigorously on his churchwarden. Voltaire was disappointed. He knew the man well—a dull fellow, none other than George III of England; well intentioned without a doubt, but one whose conversation could best be described as plodding.

"Morning," said the King when he had his pipe going to his satisfaction. "Bit cold for the time of the year, to my fancy. Help the turnips though. Touch of frost in April is good for turnips."

Voltaire sighed. The last thing he wanted to talk about was turnips, and the last person he wanted to talk to was this dull English king. He nodded, sat down, and picked up a copy of the *Paradise Gazette*, partly in self-defense and partly in the hope of finding among the list of new arrivals a familiar name. There was none. There were columns of Smiths, Joneses, Browns, Greens, and their French, Italian, German, Chinese, and African equivalents. Their occupations on earth were listed as automobile mechanic (whatever that was), bus driver, schoolteacher, bartender, literary critic (that surprised Voltaire), and so on. But there was not a single name familiar

21

to Voltaire either personally or by reputation, and he turned to the correspondence columns.

Here matters were quite as dull—a letter from one called Schoenberg (the exchange had been going on for days) in praise of noise as a form of music, and another from an impossible Jesuit, Teilhard de Chardin, who had got himself hopelessly befuddled between the Grace of God and what he called oogenesis.

Voltaire turned to the Astrology column. This, a favorite among the saints, was printed with the warning over the top that it had got the Babylonians into a lot of trouble and was for the amusement of readers only. Born November 21, Voltaire came under the sign of Aquarius the Water Carrier and was admonished to look for a remarkable change and to exercise charity to others—even those he did not like.

He glanced at the English king and said, "When were you born?" The King, without removing the stem of the churchwarden from his mouth, said, "June fourth, New Style. May twenty-fourth, Old Style. Damned nuisance. Never could get it straight. I had a couple of aunts who swore the New Style was just a Papist plot to cheat the world out of eleven days of good living, and they followed the Old Style. You were a Papist, weren't you?"

"Ummmmmmmmmm," said Voltaire. "That is not a general view."

"Fellow should know what he is; what he stands for," said the King. "Church of England through and through myself and be damned to the rest of them for a pack of whining Whigs. I was right too. I'm here, they're not. Haven't met a Whig since I arrived." He turned on for a while about Whigs, and Voltaire, bored, settled down behind the *Gazette*. The King, finding he aroused no interest in the Frenchman, glanced about the reading room and spotted the clock standing in a corner and almost merged into the shadows.

"Hello," he said. "What's this?" And then, answering his

own question, he exclaimed, "A clock! By George! A clock. Never saw one here before." He trundled over to it, and Voltaire, interested, glanced over the top of his paper at him.

"Doesn't work," said the King, who, reaching the clock, put one ear close to the case and noted that there wasn't any "tick." "Doesn't work. Extraordinary thing. What's it here for anyway?" And without waiting for an answer he seized the bellpull and rang for the porter who normally attended guests in the reading room during the day. But it was not the porter who answered his ring but a very pretty angel dressed in a miniskirt which drew an appreciative glance from Voltaire.

"Charming," he said, and the angel glanced at him and smiled.

"Thank you, dear brother," she replied.

Voltaire frowned. " 'Dear brother,' " he repeated. "What a depressing relationship. Couldn't it be something er . . . something else?"

"We are all brothers and sisters in Heaven," said the angel primly.

"A pity," said Voltaire. "A pity."

"What about the clock?" demanded the King. "What's it doing here?" He pointed to it, and the angel moved over to it curiously.

"What is it?" she asked.

"A clock," said the King. "I've just told you."

"What's a clock?" asked the angel.

"It's a thing for telling time with," replied the King. "They are always wrong. In my palace I had a fellow called the Royal Cock Crower who came around every hour and went 'Cock-a-doodle-doo. It's one o'clock' or whatever it was. I'd have discharged him except that he had a wife and family to support, and he couldn't do anything else. So I kept him."

"That was kind of you," said the angel and kissed the King on his cheek. Voltaire, slightly envious, recalled an act of even greater kindness on his part as he saw it. "My dear," he said, "I distinctly recall reading Rousseau's *Le Contrat Social* and not flinging it out of the window. That was very kind of me. Don't I get anything?"

"No," said the angel. "You cannot be kind to a book. You have to be kind to people." She turned to look at the clock again, quite fascinated by it, and said to Voltaire, "What is time?"

"Come, *chérie*," he said, seeing an opportunity, "you have asked precisely the right person, and I will explain everything to you. It is very simple and at the same time, very complicated. By the way, what is your name?"

"Cecile."

"Cecile," said Voltaire. "Entrancing. It suits you like a flower." He seated her in a chair and drew up another beside her, but not before the King, who entertained deep suspicions of all Frenchmen, had seated himself on the other side.

"You have to watch him," said the King. "Literary type. It makes them devious. They can't say anything plain and straightforward. Now time is . . . time is . . ."

"Time is what?" challenged Voltaire.

"Very simple," said the King. "Time is measured on clocks, and clocks are for measuring time. That's all anybody needs to know about it."

"Excellent," said Voltaire. "If you do not understand something—just give it a name. That's all that's necessary."

"I'm afraid I *still* don't understand," said Cecile. She turned to Voltaire. "Could you explain, dear brother?" she asked.

"Dear brother," said Voltaire with a sigh. "Certainly . . . dear sister." Cecile had put her hands in her lap, and Voltaire reached out and took them. "So tiny," he said. "As lovely as a carving in ivory. Once, *chérie*, I remember just such a one as you. In the shadow of the elms by Notre Dame. There was half a moon and one white hand—which I held so." He raised

24

the hand slowly to his lips and the King shouted, "Time! Voltaire. Time!"

"What in the name of Heaven is this?" cried Voltaire, outraged. "A boxing match?"

"You were going to explain Time to our dear sister," said the King.

"Is it something like hate?" asked Cecile, not in the slightest put out. "That's another thing I can't understand."

"No," said Voltaire recovering himself. "Time is not like hate. Love and hate are eternal. But time has a beginning and an end. Time is change, and change is dissatisfaction or imperfection. Nothing that is perfect ever changes, but whatever is imperfect seeks perfection; moves toward it as best it can, and to do so has to live in time. Do you understand?"

"I think so," said Cecile.

"Well, I don't," said the King. "You haven't said a word about clocks."

The angel undertook to explain. "Whatever is perfect is quite still and eternal," she said. "And whatever is not perfect is changing and moving toward perfection and that's called Time. How beautifully simple. But then everything about God is simple. You understand Him better than most of us, dear brother."

"That's because I argued with him," said Voltaire. "The first step toward understanding is of course argument. An argument is, in fact, a form of a love affair, leading toward knowledge and intimacy."

"Nonsense," snorted King George. "Are you going to tell me that wars are merely love affairs; that when the English line met the French line at Fontenoy, the slaughter that followed was the equivalent of a damned minuet? That my struggle against those confounded rebellious, hell-inspired American colonists was a mere flirtation? Piffle, sir. Downright piffle. I'd have hanged that fellow Washington myself if I

25

could have got my hands on him. Well, we all know where *he* is."

"Yes, indeed," said Cecile.

"Serves him right," said the King. "Serves him right. I'll never understand the fellow. Just to think that with all the benefits of a thoroughly British background—plenty of exercise in the open air—not too much reading—and so on; with all those benefits he should turn against his own sovereign and challenge the Divine Right of Kings. Think of it. He was almost an Englishman—yes—almost an Englishman. And he turned on England. Why, that's like turning against Nature itself."

Faintly from outside The Club, when the King had finished, came a shout of "Hallelujah" from Handel's famous chorus, with below it, forming a descant, the opening bars of "Rule Britannia."

Voltaire was intrigued.

Chapter Three

Voltaire and George III left The Club without discovering why the clock had been brought there, and when they had gone the porter waited to see who would be the next to discover it, for he was curious himself as to why he had been ordered to fetch it from Earth and might get some hint from the identity of the saints who discovered it. The next two surprised him—none other than the Americans, Saint Thomas Jefferson and Saint George Washington. They clattered up the driveway to The Club on steaming horses.

They were both soaking wet, for they had been indulging in their favorite sport—hard cross-country riding in a pelting rain, hedges and ditches taken without mercy, streams jumped or galloped through with a great splashing of hooves; uphill and downdale, helter-skelter as fast as man and beast could go. Washington had a big white Irish hunter, with a stride so easy that riding it was like sitting in a rocking chair, but Jefferson had a chestnut mare, with a touch of Arab in her breeding—high spirited and at times a little nervous. He called the mare Congress.

The two reined up in a hail of loose gravel and, dismounting, threw the reins to stable hands. "Give them a good rubdown," said Jefferson. "See that the mare doesn't get cold."

"Let's get in to the fire ourselves," said Washington. "These boots of mine are so wet they'll take half an hour to get off. I can almost taste that whiskey punch."

27

They clumped into the reading room and, flinging off their wet riding coats, went immediately to the fire, Washington pausing only to ring the bellpull for punch. "Gad," he said when this had arrived, "nothing I like more than a hard gallop through rain. Stirs up the bile. Makes your blood run. Cleans out your lungs. Best thing in the world for a man." He took a sniff of the whiskey punch which had been brought by the porter and said with a chuckle, "It was the death of me, you know, Tom. Caught an inflammation of the lungs or something and though they bled me white, I died."

"I know," said Jefferson thoughtfully. "When I heard the news I was—profoundly affected. Profoundly."

Washington smacked his lips cheerfully and said, "Ungentlemanly thing, dying. Upsets so many people. You'd think they could arrange it some other way—so as not to be a damned nuisance. That's the trouble with dying in your own bed—more considerate to arrange to go away somewhere if one could. In my case, I didn't have a chance. I didn't know I was going to die."

"Tell me," said Jefferson earnestly. "When you *did* know you were going to die—what did you think about? What did you have on your mind?"

"Discounting what I thought of the doctor?" asked Washington.

"Yes."

"Well, the Hundred Acre for one thing."

"The Hundred Acre?"

"Yes, the big field to the north of Mount Vernon, bordering the woods. That field defeated me. Too wet for tobacco. Too sour for beans. Barley wouldn't thrive there nor wheat nor corn. Useless for turnips and gave only a rough pasture. There was a pan of granite below or perhaps slate, and all the ingenuity of man couldn't drain it." He fell silent, musing on the problem. Then, recalling that his riding boots were wet, he clumped over to an easy chair and started to remove

28

them, straining back and putting the toe of one against the heel of the other in an attempt to pry the boot loose.

"What else?" asked Jefferson.

"Eh?"

"What else?"

"Oh, the King," said Washington still struggling with his boots.

"The King?" cried Jefferson in surprise.

"Yes. The King. I don't mean his miserable ministers— Bute, Townshend, North, and the rest of them. Pack of blackguards. I wouldn't hire them for stable hands. They'd steal the horses' oats. But the King . . ."

"The King, sir, was a tyrant," exploded Jefferson. "The King was a despot, the enemy of freedom of any sort unless granted by himself, and that is not freedom but privilege. Freedom is not in the gift of any man, to be given or withheld upon a whim—a reward to obedient dogs for good behavior." He grew quite hot thinking of it. "Freedom, sir," he cried, "is as common to men as is air, sunlight, and water. And the greatest foe of freedom in your lifetime and mine was always and in every aspect that bestial monarch George the Third."

Washington continued to struggle with his boots through this, but mumbled, "You certainly hated him, Tom."

"I didn't hate him at all," retorted Jefferson. "Indeed, I never met him. I detested his principles. That is all."

"My father drank the King's health every evening," said Washington. "And I drank it many a time. Wore the King's coat in the Virginia militia too. I'll tell you this—I never thought to turn on the King—never."

"Turn on him?" cried Jefferson. "It was he who turned on us. The King was a pigheaded, dull-minded tyrant who attained power by accident of birth and retained it by every parliamentary villainy imaginable."

Washington gave up the struggle with his boots for the

moment. "Died mad, poor fellow," he said. "They used to put him in a maze in Hampton Court, I'm told, and leave him there all day. He couldn't find his way out until the attendants came to fetch him. He mumbled away to himself, thinking he was talking to Frederick of Prussia and his queen, long dead, and playing games with his fingers, they say. I've heard they sometimes forgot him and left him there, and he would be shivering with cold in the dark when they remembered him—like a dog left out of doors."

Jefferson was not moved. "Very regrettable," he said loftily. "Very regrettable. But it is highly possible that those who oppose themselves determinedly to the natural rights of man become mad, and King George the Third may be but one of history's classic examples of just such a result." Jefferson had by now, his legs being slimmer, managed to remove his own riding boots, which he placed neatly to one side of the fire. He came over to Washington, who was still struggling, and said, "Your boots are still too wet. They will come off easier if you'll dry them by the fire and let the leather enlarge itself."

"Damn it, Tom," said Washington testily, "I've been taking off riding boots, man and boy, for forty years, and I don't need lessons from you now. I like to fight 'em. When you get 'em off, the feeling of triumph is tremendous."

Jefferson smiled and returned to the fire. In doing so, he noticed the clock standing in the corner of the room. "Hello," he said in surprise. "What's this?" and going over to it, he examined it with pleasure for he had loved clocks on earth. "Look," he said. "A clock. I haven't seen one in—I don't know how long."

Washington, who had now succeeded in getting off one boot, turned around and then clumped over to the clock, one boot on, one boot off. It seemed vaguely familiar.

"That's my old clock," he cried. "It isn't working." He opened the clock case and glanced inside.

"No pendulum," he said. "That's why."

30

"No. That's not it," said Jefferson thoughtfully. "There's no time in eternity. That's why it isn't working."

"Well, why have the thing here?" said Washington.

"I don't know," said Jefferson. "But I do know that nothing happens without a reason."

"Makes a good effect," said Washington. "The wall looked a little bare without it."

Jefferson shook his head. "No," he said. "Something deeper than that. A clock measures time. And there is no time here. So why would it be here at all?"

He stared at it, puzzled and vaguely apprehensive.

Chapter Four

On an ottoman in the reading room, Benjamin Franklin was taking a nap. He did so every noon, and nobody ever took any notice of him. He had a handkerchief over his face to keep off the flies for he could not accustom himself to the idea that the flies in Heaven had strict instructions not to annoy sleepers. The word *clock* intruded on his dreams. He woke, grunting a little, removed the handkerchief, and fumbled about for his glasses. Then he said in his flat, New England voice, "Did someone say, 'clock'?"

"Yes," said Jefferson. "There's one here! Do you know who brought it?"

Franklin, without replying, ambled over to the clock and, his hands behind his back, examined it minutely. He stooped to inspect the bottom part. He stood on tiptoe to look at the dial. He looked at the sides as carefully as the front, and then he opened the door in the front of it and peered inside the case, and noted, as had the others, that there was no pendulum. He did not comment on this but walked to the bellpull by the fireplace and gave it a jerk.

The porter, Gabriel, who had been peeking through the door and observing all this, had instructions not to answer the bell. It was answered instead by a pretty maid dressed in a long gown with a high waistline, and a ribbon cap in the style of the latter part of the eighteenth century. She was, to judge by the innocence and loveliness of her face, about sixteen or seventeen years of age, and Franklin walked to her, both hands outstretched as if welcoming a friend.

"Not the Countess Marie des Petits Chalons?" he said.

"Ah, no sir," she replied, dropping him a curtsy. "My name is Ruth. I am an angel."

"So was she—an angel," said Franklin. "A child, with a title going back to the Flood, I suppose. She used to visit me often in Paris with her little problems and she called me Poo Poo."

"Why?" asked the angel.

"She had from childhood a stuffed bear—it was blue—of which she was very fond. She said I reminded her of it. Poor little thing," he added. "They cut off her head, and she didn't know what it was all about." He turned and looked at Jefferson, the clock forgotten for the moment. "Revolutions," he said. "Revolutions. Revolutions to free the masses. Revolutions to free the mind. Do you suppose, Tom, that there are as many innocent victims of revolutions as there are of the tyrannies they seek to overthrow?"

"Quite probably," said Jefferson. "The Tree of Liberty must regularly receive a good drench of blood to prosper—blood is its manure."

"My poor little Countess Marie," said Franklin. "Manure for the Tree of Liberty. I trust some lovely blossoms grew from her." He turned again to the angel and asked, "You are sure you are not she?"

"Quite sure," said the angel. "But did you call for me?"

"Yes," said Franklin. "This clock here—do you know who brought it and why it was brought here?"

"No, sir," said the angel. "I don't."

"You've had no hint?" asked Jefferson.

"What's a hint?" asked the angel.

"It's a suggestion leading, at times, to knowledge," replied Franklin.

Ruth shook her head. "We angels either know or we don't know. There is nothing between," she said.

"You haven't heard anybody else talk about it?" asked Washington, who was now, his boots removed, gratefully in his stocking feet.

"One of my sister angels, Cecile, said she heard some of the saints discussing it. They said it is called a clock. They said it was neither love nor hate, which are immortal, but Time which is perishable. But I do not understand what Time is or what perishable is."

"You say other saints were talking to your sister Cecile about it?" said Franklin. "What saints?"

"I didn't ask their names," she said. "But my sister Cecile said that one of the saints was a French saint who quarreled with the Lord often on Earth, and the other was an English saint who always did what the Lord expected him to do."

The three of them reflected on this information, and Washington remarked wryly that one of the troubles of belonging to the Established Church was that you learned a great deal about clergy and nothing about saints. But Jefferson, who prided himself on his knowledge of France, said, "A French saint would likely be Saint Denis, who was once a king of France and is indeed its patron. And an English saint might be Saint George—though I've heard that actually he was a Greek or a Turk or an Armenian."

"Saint George," cried Washington with enthusiasm. "Saint George? Now why didn't I think of him before? Just fancy, Tom. Splendid horseman and one of the world's greatest hunters. Dragons, Tom. Reflect on that. Dragons. And we spent our time halloaing after foxes. I'd very much like to meet Saint George."

"Really?" said Angel Ruth. "Oh, I'm sure that can be easily arranged."

34

Chapter Five

Lieutenant Tom Czeuleger of the United States Marines was a trifle confused. He had found a wonderful new girl friend, Jennie, the Social Secretary to the President, and he had also discovered that she was either an atrocious liar or the simple-minded dupe of subversives—though when he thought of her pleasant face, her attractive figure, her open and direct manner, that seemed rank heresy.

He had finished the inventory of the furniture in her office, but he had been completely unable to discover the whereabouts of the grandfather clock she said had been taken away by a messenger from the clockmaker. The address given —3333 Circle Drive—didn't exist. There was a 3331 and a 3335 but no 3333, and there never had been. The lady who lived in 3331 had lived there twenty years and stated there was no clockmaker anywhere in the area. Nor was there a porter or a messenger by the name of A. A. Gabriel living anywhere nearby, or in the employ of any trucking company or messenger service in the area.

He went over Jennie's dossier carefully, for in any investigation he knew it was folly to presume that anyone was innocent. He checked in it her grade school record, her high school record, her college record, her church affiliation, her hobbies, her credit cards, her credit accounts, her bank balances, her political affiliations, meetings she had attended, clubs she had belonged to or been associated with, her friends, outings, social occasions, holidays and where spent—all the details which in that land devoted to freedom for all the government feels it is essential to have on each of its citizens seeking government service.

Her bank account had been overdrawn on four occasions during her college years, but never by more than five dollars. She had had a tuition scholarship at college, and her parents had paid for her board. She had lived on campus. She had driven an old Chevy sedan, had had no extravagant tastes, hardly drank at all, was not a drug user, gave blood once a year to the Red Cross. . . . The only dubious detail in the whole of her college record was that she had studied political science.

"Why couldn't she have studied English Literature instead?" said Tom, who had assembled all these details to give to his new boss, Ted Storhill, over in the Treasury Department.

That, of course, was the one detail that Storhill picked on. "Political science, eh?" he said.

"Probably taught by some Joe who couldn't raise ten bucks for a wounded Boy Scout. Who was her professor?"

"Edwards. Clinton E. Edwards."

"Never heard of him," said Storhill, "but run a check on him anyway. The immediate problem, however, is that clock. No trace of the man she says came for it?"

"None at all."

"There's something fishy about this whole thing," said Storhill. "He was an older guy, you say, and took the clock out of the window. Now how is an old man going to hassle that thing off the terrace to a driveway forty yards away, which was the nearest place he could get a truck. And nobody saw him—or the truck."

Tom said nothing. He'd asked himself all these questions before.

"What happened to that truck?" continued Storhill.

"They're all checked in. They're all checked out. You've been over the whole list of entries and exits for that day, and there was no truck or van with an old man and a grandfather clock in it. Be pretty hard to miss a grandfather clock, you know."

"That gate check isn't as good as it ought to be," said Tom. "The Marine guards just look at the driver's pass and let him in and out. They don't actually go through every vehicle unless they have a reason to do so. There were a number of panel truckes that just might have had the grandfather clock in the back.

"The real point is that it doesn't matter so much about the grandfather clock's leaving the White House. The important thing is to prevent its getting back again without being inspected. Actually I really can't believe that there's any threat in this thing. I mean a grandfather clock is a bit far out for a bomb-timer. There are a hundred other things far less conspicuous and far more efficient."

"Like what?" asked Storhill.

"Well, like a telephone," said Tom. "You could rig a telephone so that when it rang a certain number of rings it blew up, or when you picked up the receiver it blew up, or when you dialed a particular number it blew up. So why use a grandfather clock?"

"Because the President's telephones are checked daily," said Storhill. "And who checks a grandfather clock? What about this A. A. Gabriel? You say he wore campaign ribbons? Have you checked him through veterans' lists?"

"There's a lot of Gabriels," said Tom. "I'm checking everything, but I just don't believe that there's anything to it. I know this girl personally and well—I just don't believe there's any kind of a plot involved."

When Tom had gone Storhill thoughtfully picked up the telephone and said, "Send Evans in." Evans, a heavyset man wearing an old-fashioned gray flannel suit, plodded through the door. He was one of the slowest men on the Secret Service staff, but he had the supreme virtue of being eminently thorough and without personal affiliations of any kind.

"I want you to go over the dossier of Lieutenant Tom Czeuleger of the United States Marine Corps," said Storhill. "He's been loaned to us and is working on a case right now. Find out all about his background and find out who he's seen with, who he talks to, what telephone calls he makes—everything he does all day and every day until further orders. Find out whether he likes girls generally or just one girl or boys or whatever. Find out if he's a potential subject for blackmail. Oh, and find out whether he ever studied political science at the University of Southern Vermont under a guy called Clinton E. Edwards."

When Evans had gone Storhill again picked up the phone and asked for another man to be sent in, and this one was instructed to investigate Clinton E. Edwards, professor of political science. Two hours later, at lunch with a member of the Senate Finance Committee, Storhill expressed his sober belief that in no country in the world were its citizens freer in every aspect of their living than in the United States of America, but added that he was going to need a considerable increase in his budget for wiretapping so as to keep it that way.

Tom had a date with Jennie two days later, but it turned into a miserable affair. He kept wondering whether she was a dupe or he was a dupe. They parted coldly, and he suspected that another date would be hard to arrange and perhaps had better not be arranged at all until the mystery of the grandfather clock had been cleared up.

Chapter Six

Meanwhile in Heaven Martha Washington was chatting with her best friend, Queen Charlotte, who on Earth had been the wife of George III of England. The thoughtful will not be surprised at this, for the strange bedfellows allowed to politicians on Earth are mirrored by the strange companionships permitted to the saved in Heaven. The two had met in the same rose garden, for on Earth they had both been very fond of flowers, and Martha Washington had often received gifts of rose slips and tulip bulbs (tulips, a Dutch fancy to start with, were all the rage in those days) from Jefferson. Each was well aware of the other's identity, and a certain delicacy had prevented them from ever discussing the whereabouts of their husbands. It was a subject to be avoided at all costs.

The two ladies, then, stuck to neutral topics—the management of servants, the layout of gardens, the need for larger closets in every household, the supervision of kitchens, and the danger of drafts. They were discussing drafts now, for it was a favorite topic with them, and they carried shawls lest a draft should be met with even in Paradise.

"The Palace was the draftiest place on Earth," said the Queen. "There was need for a screen around every chair in every room to be able to rest in comfort. And poor George suffered terribly from catarrh, though I really think that was the result of pipe smoking."

"It is strange, isn't it?" said Martha reflectively. "Your husband smoked tobacco, and my husband grew tobacco. And yet . . ."

"*Smoked* tobacco," said the Queen. "Why, between his pipe and his snuff he practically lived on tobacco. He was so angry when that man went up that river and burned all the tobacco warehouses somewhere."

"That was Jamestown in Virginia," said Martha.

"Jamestown in Virginia?" echoed the Queen, quite surprised. "Well, fancy. I always thought the way George talked of it that Jamestown was in England—somewhere near Portsmouth."

"That was part of the trouble," said Martha a trifle stiffly.

"Well, the whole thing was very silly," said the Queen. "Just like men. They really needed each other, and so they had to quarrel. I mean my George loved tobacco and your George produced it, and then they both liked farming, and if they'd just met each other they would have got on famously. My George was very easy to get along with—provided you let him have his head."

"So was mine," said Martha Washington. "But he flew into a terrible temper if he thought anyone was working against him. Once he turned on Jefferson in such a way that I thought they would never speak to each other again. Accused him of slandering him and undermining his position and everything. It was just dreadful."

"Exactly what the King did with Pitt," said Queen Charlotte. "He raged for days. Said that his name predicted his end and all kinds of horrible things."

"Well," said Martha Washington, "they can never meet now." There was a tinge of sadness in her voice that went right to the heart of the Queen.

"There there, my dear," she said, taking her hand and patting it. "Just don't think about it. I'm sure that where he is he'll—he'll get used to it."

"Get used to it?" cried Martha Washington. "Why, he

40

enjoys every moment of it. He does precisely what he wants. The last time I saw him he'd been riding all morning in the rain with Mr. Jefferson. He *loves* riding in the rain."

"Rain?" said the Queen a trifle dubiously. "I hardly thought that it rained where Mr. Washington is. That's not the official description."

"What do you mean—the official description?" asked the other.

"The description authorized by the Church of England, of course, which carries the full sanction of Parliament. That description says—well—that it's very hot there."

"Where?" demanded Mrs. Washington.

"You know perfectly well where I mean," said the Queen bridling. "It's not ladylike to mention the name."

"I'd have you know that Mr. Washington, having done his duty to his country, is right here with me in Heaven," said Martha testily. "Whereas your husband . . ."

"And I'd have you know," said the Queen, "that my husband, having done his duty to God and to his people, is right here in Heaven too."

They stared at each other, amazed and a little more than a trifle dubious.

"Can this be possible?" they said together. Then Martha Washington, turning back up the path down which they had been strolling, and Queen Charlotte, looking in the other direction, both called out, "George." And from the two ends of the path came George Washington, tall and reserved, and George III, stubby and a trifle out of breath. They glanced at each other, a trifle suspiciously, awaiting an introduction, and each said to his spouse, "You called, my dear."

The two ladies hesitated for only a second Then Martha Washington, taking the Queen's hand, said, "It's high time that you two met and settled your differences face to face. Mr. Washington, I would like you to meet George the Third, King of England."

41

Across the great vault of Heaven there came on the moment a deep roll of thunder, and one of the wyverns, who had just leaped into the sky to exclaim, "Gloria in excelsis Deo" in an excess of joy, fell back to the ground among the lilies of the field—speechless.

Chapter Seven

Voltaire had a wide acquaintanceship in Heaven. Those who had died after him were aware of his fame on Earth; and once they had overcome their initial joy (and in some cases surprise) at being there themselves, they looked about for others who were not known for singing Hallelujahs during their mortal life. Among those they found, Voltaire was a prize, and he had had many lively exchanges with Schopenhauer about Will, and Nietzsche about Power, and Shaw about Socialism, and with Camus (who lent him a copy) about *La Peste*.

"The book is not concerned with the plague itself," Camus explained, "but with philosophical and theological subtleties. As for instance whether, as the Jesuit maintained, God could indeed visit such a terrible affliction as bubonic plague on Man for his own good."

"My dear Camus," Voltaire replied, "a pity you should have wasted your talents on a subject which I dealt with myself two centuries earlier in a little book called *Candide*. But perhaps my modest work escaped your attention."

Voltaire also counted among his friends such notables as Locke, Spinoza, Hobbes, Descartes, Duns Scotus, and Aquinas, and, among the early Arabs, al-Kindi and Averroës, and others.

The two great protagonists of differing theories of government—George III and George Washington—having been brought together in Heaven, Voltaire, as soon as he heard of it, decided that nothing could be more stimulating and informative and perhaps even amusing than to have the two debate their respective positions before a brilliant assemblage of the greatest minds Earth had ever produced.

The debate was not difficult to arrange. An announcement about it was printed in the *Gazette* and all who were interested in theories of human freedom and the government of man were invited to attend. Voltaire himself would be moderator.

They turned up in droves—not only philosophers A.D. but philosophers B.C. There were Platonists and Neoplatonists and Epicureans and Stoics and Skeptics and Eclectics in charming variety, and also Nihilists and Positivists and Materialists and Pantheists and Panphysicists, Existentialists and Transcendentalists, Behaviorists, and Realists and Pragmatists, and Humanists, and when the porter saw them all crowding into the reading room on the day appointed, he called management for more help, anticipating trouble.

Things started off quietly enough, however. Everybody was very friendly and courteous. All crowded together in the reading room while more and more streamed in until there was hardly room for the angels to pass about with canapes of ambrosia and a glass or two of Pinot Grand Fenwick or other heavenly wine. But then a discussion started between the Stoics and the Pragmatists on the subject of Power and Will.

The Stoic view of gentlemanly acceptance of whatever happened ran directly counter to that of the followers of Nietzsche that man should and could shape his own fate. The argument became less polite, firmer, more assertive, and then definitely heated. It did not get out of hand, but it stimulated other discussions among other groups. And soon Existentialists and Positivists, Platonists and Behaviorists were going at it. Voices became louder, fingers were waved, and then fists and arms.

The porter, hearing the hubbub, was reminded of the first meeting of its kind at a place called Babel; and Voltaire, banging away with his gavel on the table, in an endeavor to establish order, was unable to get anyone to pay the slightest attention to him.

"Gentlemen. Gentlemen!" he shouted but without effect, and at last Washington plucked at his arm and said in his ear, "It is easier to halt grenadiers in mid-charge than philosophers in mid-debate. Let us adjourn to the terrace." So out they went and there found a little man with a round face and a button of a nose, his bald pate ringed with curls, dressed in the flowing robes of an Athenian.

"Ah, my dear Socrates," said Voltaire. "You alone of all of us were wise enough not to attend such a meeting."

"Not a bit of it," said Socrates. "I would have been in there with the rest of them, but Xanthippe wouldn't let me."

Such was the hubbub that, around the wall of The Club, the various beasts of Paradise were gathered, peeping over in consternation. "See what comes of eating the fruit of that terrible Tree of Knowledge," said a noble unicorn to his little fawns gathered around him. "Madness and a loss of all grace and nobility. Let that be a lesson to you."

But Voltaire, with a contemptuous glance at the frightened animals, said, "Mere beasts. Let us get down to our work." He found a table and chairs in a quiet spot of the terrace and, having seated the two Georges and Jefferson and Franklin, who were in attendance, himself sat between them and asked the King to first state his point of view.

"It must have dawned on you gentlemen," he said, "that you both being here—no doubt to your mutual surprise—the conclusion is inevitable that neither of you was wrong—either that or Someone made a mistake. Which I am assured is impossible."

45

"I am here," said George III, "because invested by God with the authority which is given to kings alone—the authority which is summed up in the phrase, 'The Divine Right of Kings'—I at all times did my duty to the people entrusted by God to my care. And you, sir," he said, turning to Washington, "are here through the mercy of God. It can be for no other reason."

Washington said, with a touch of sarcasm, "Such conviction must have been a great comfort to you, sir. For myself . . ." He broke off.

"Yes," said the King. "For yourself—what?"

"For myself, I will frankly confess that there were times when all my resolution seemed to fail, when misfortune piling upon misfortune, doubts tore at me like devils leaping out of the darkness to bear me down. Five hundred dead here —a thousand there. This village burned. This city taken. Boston relieved but Philadelphia occupied. New York Tory to the man and my troops unfed and ill-clad in the bitterest cold I recall in all my years. Yes indeed, there were times to try men's souls.

"Yet at the worst of times I was given a sign—as it were from Heaven. A run of shad up the river when I had but a dozen barrels of weevily corn to feed two thousand men at Morristown. And then de Grasse coming in from nowhere off the capes of the Chesapeake. And so on. At the worst of times, when all seemed blackest, there was always a ray of light, and in the end we won."

"You won," said the King, "because of the interference of the pestilential French. But it is the heaviest possible charge against you, that you, who were almost an Englishman, first raised in the world the horrid specter of Republicanism which was later to sweep France, destroying an order a thousand years old. It was you who first taught men in their governments to set aside the will of God and substitute for it the will of the people."

"Good heavens, sir," exploded Washington, "can you really sit there and insist that you believe that you as King of England represented the will of God?"

"I can and I do," said George.

"Fiddlesticks," exploded Jefferson. "In the area of politics, God is unconcerned."

Washington turned on him a look of astonishment but Voltaire said smoothly, "Privilege, gentlemen. Privilege. The debate is privileged. We may say what we please quite freely. But as chairman of the debate I would like to put a point to His Majesty. I trust I have your permission?"

The King grunted, a trifle suspicious.

"My point is a simple one, but to clear the ground I would first ask whether you still assert that kings are divinely appointed."

"That is fundamental," said George. "You will find full warrant for it in the Bible in the anointing of Saul."

"So the king in his relation to his people is the agent of God?" asked Voltaire.

"That is so."

"And this cannot be true of one king but must be true of all?"

"Elementary," said George, and Socrates, who had been sitting with his back to a post, turned his head slightly toward the group and grinned.

"If then," said Voltaire, "all kings are divinely appointed and are the agents of God on Earth, why does the King of England fight the King of France and the King of Finland fight the King of Sweden? Are they not all agents, as you say, of the same God?"

"Because," said George, his face a touch of purple, "the King of France is a damned fool, and so is the King of Finland and the King of Sweden."

"I hadn't thought of that," mumbled Socrates. "But after all, it is possible."

"The fact of the matter is," said Jefferson testily, "that the principle of kingship is opposed to all reason. It assumes that there is more sense and experience and understanding in one man's head than there is in the heads of a thousand or indeed of a million. And that this sense is handed down through hundreds of years from father to son. Such a conclusion cannot be countenanced for one moment."

"One moment," said Franklin, who had seated himself close to Socrates and a little away from the others, "I have served on many committees and on many legislatures in my lifetime. I have to confess that I have never come across a brilliant committee or a gifted legislature, whereas there are many brilliant and gifted men. In short, it could be argued that the republican mode can reproduce only what is mediocre and commonplace—and the fruits of democracy may be caution, inaction, and procrastination."

"Sir," said Jefferson a trifle stiffly, "you sound as though you favor the royal form of government."

"My friend," replied Franklin gently, "I am not a very wise man but I have learned not to favor one form over another until I have learned all I can about them all. We knew in our day what was to be said on one side and on the other. But we do not know how our venture into the republican form, which astonished the world in our time, came out. We saw only the start. We do not know what was the result."

"The result, sir?" said the King. "The result could have been nothing but disaster and that for reasons plain to any man of sense."

"I would be glad to hear your reasons," said Washington.

"So you shall," said the King. "In the first place you must acknowledge that you rebelled against your legitimate and natural government and you called in the enemies of that government to succeed in your rebellion, for you could not

48

have succeeded without the aid of the King's enemies . . ."

"Sir," cried Jefferson, but the King silenced him with a wave of his chubby hand.

"By succeeding in your rebellion against your legitimate government with the aid of the enemies of that government, you set an example for the whole world to follow for generations to come. You proclaimed to people everywhere the right to rebel against their governments."

"To our eternal credit," cried Jefferson.

"Indeed," said the King. "And how long do you think your own government could last with such a principle established? Does it not occur to you that the right to rebel having once been sanctioned must, in the nature of things, produce chaos, rebellion following on rebellion, each government established being overthrown by dissenters and so on and on until all must end in disaster? You overthrew the natural order ordained by God and substituted government by rebels. Why then, sir, were we to return now, we would surely either find all in ruin, or the rule of kings restored, not only in America but throughout the Earth."

"Sir," said Washington, "you make a fundamental error. It is this. Rebellion is not a natural state with men. Men rebel only when there is no other remedy for their ills. Under the republican form they have adequate representation for the adjustment of grievances without resort to arms. Therefore the republican form, rather than the royal form, is the more lasting and the more reasonable, and being the more conducive to peace and the less conducive to dissatisfaction, must surely at this time be the established form all over the Earth."

To this George replied that the republican form merely set up a thousand tyrants where previously there had been at most but one; that a man might petition a king for redress but how was he to petition a Congress?

49

So the argument went on until between the King talking about duty and Jefferson about the pursuit of happiness, Voltaire got a headache and, what was worse, became bored.

The whole confrontation, which should have been brilliant, deteriorated at length into a sorry reiteration of time-worn attitudes.

"Alas," he said to Franklin, "it is plain to me now that it is not great issues that produce great debates, but great debaters. However much sense our two Georges have, neither can claim much agility of mind or command of language."

"You should not make the error," said Franklin mildly, "of mistaking actors for lawmakers. Their functions are entirely different. But I see that the debate within has quietened down."

So it had. In fact all the disputing philosophers had left The Club to think out counterarguments to the arguments which had been advanced against them, and by rooting around in their store of Inferences, Judgments, Propositions, Beliefs, Premises, Syllogisms, Hypotheses, Dilemmas, Fallacies, Paradoxes, and Analogies to come up with something that had the appearance of thought, if lacking in worth.

Only the porter remained in the reading room, straightening a table here and a chair there, and the gentlemen returned from the terrace, dissatisfied and irritated that the proof of their convictions and assertions could not be produced.

Within, they did not continue their discussion, which had thoroughly exhausted them. Voltaire attempted a summing up but concluded that while in theory there seemed to be as much to say on one side as on the other and while royal government had a far longer history upon Earth than any other form, and a fairly successful history on the whole, yet they could none of them return to Earth to find out how matters had turned out.

"We are separated by a gap which only angels can cross, he said. "We live in Eternity, Earth in Time. We cannot get from Eternity to Time and so there is nothing left for us to do but to cultivate our gardens . . ."

He was interrupted by a curious whirring noise from the corner of the reading room where the clock still stood. All turned in its direction. They were astonished to see the hands of the clock moving through the hours around the dial. They halted at last and eleven clear strokes rang out. In the silence of the room, when the last chime had died away, they could hear a solemn ticking.

"What does this mean?" cried King George.

"It means," said Voltaire, "that Time has returned to us. We may reenter it if we wish . . . if we dare."

Washington was the first to respond. He went over to the clock and opened the door of the pendulum case as if to enter.

Jefferson gripped him by the arm. "What do you propose?" he asked almost in a whisper.

"I propose to return to Earth if I can," said Washington.

"It may be terrible," said Jefferson. "It may be disastrous for all to which you gave your life, and the way back quite unsure."

"I still wish to know," said Washington calmly. "I cannot affect disinterest. That cause lies dearest of all things to my heart." His wife, Martha, with Queen Charlotte had entered the room, looking for them.

"Come, my dear," he said and gestured to the opening.

"You dare?" cried Jefferson.

"Yes," said Washington quietly, "I dare." Entering the clock, he beckoned to his wife to follow him. Jefferson, after a moment's hesitation, did the same. He was followed by King George III and his queen, leaving only Voltaire, Franklin, and Socrates in the reading room staring at the clock.

Voltaire was about to enter but, recalling something, hesitated and instead seized the bellcord by the fireplace and gave it a good ring. The angel Cecile appeared immediately.

"My dear," said Voltaire. "A wonderful opportunity has presented itself." He ushered her inside and with an elaborate bow followed her.

"And you?" said Socrates to Franklin. "Are you not also going?"

"No," said Franklin. "I know the answer already."

"You are ahead of me," said Socrates. "For I cannot say I entirely understand the question."

Chapter Eight

Voltaire was delighted with the Presidential Ball. It was just the kind of occasion that he most enjoyed; the press of beautifully groomed people about him, the lights, the excitement, the sense of being witty, brilliant, and admired, the delicious women, the handsome men, the interchange of quips and sallies and ideas, all combined to make the kind of scene that animated him and filled his life with what was intended to fill it.

He was entranced and had the feeling, quite usual with him, that the whole occasion was given in his honor, and so he moved about the crowds in his satin breeches and silk stockings, his brocaded coat and his flowered waistcoat, his magnificent wig with its waterdog curl, and his elegant staff of ebony with the top a chaste sphere of ivory as if he were king and they all there to do him homage.

The angel Cecile, on his arm, was delighted too, but with the delight of a child at its first carnival. Everyone was so happy, so gay, so colorful, and so clever that she felt particularly lucky and blessed to have been chosen as the guardian for this short time on Earth of Saint Voltaire, whose previous guardian angel had been granted a well-earned eternity of rest.

"Voyez, ma petite," said Voltaire, indicating the whole scene with a graceful sweep of a hand dripping lace. "Here

is Man in one of his best aspects—as full of lies, deceits, and intrigues as ever, but added to it all, manners, grace, and wit. How wonderful. I am sure to meet an old—er, an old acquaintance—any moment. You are permitted to be a tiny bit jealous—remember that without a little pain, a little anguish, the relations between the sexes become insupportably dull. If you are not jealous I will be very angry with you. . . ."

He was about to explain the absolute necessity for jealousy even in the slightest flirtation when someone bumped into him from behind, so violently that Voltaire clapped his hand to his waist to feel for his sword.

"Excuse me," said the man who had bumped into him. "I guess I wasn't looking where I was going. Did you ever see such a madhouse?"

Voltaire turned and examined the intruder inch by inch, starting with his shoes. When he arrived at the man's face he was dismayed to find it was young and handsome in contrast with his own, and this made him all the more icy.

The young man, who was none other than Tom Czeuleger, dressed in the uniform of a Pennsylvania militiaman of the 1780s, glanced at Cecile, who gave him such a smile of innocence and love that his heart was immediately melted.

"My name's Czeuleger," he said. "Lieutenant Tom Czeuleger."

Voltaire shrugged. The fellow obviously wasn't even worth quarreling with. "Honored, my dear sir," he said. "I am . . ."

"No, don't say," said Tom quickly. "I want to guess. You're . . . er . . . you're . . . you're Rip Van Winkle." He didn't really mean to say Rip Van Winkle. It was just a name that popped into his head through an association of ideas—the vague impression that the man before him was not only old but dressed in a style more authentically old-fashioned than all the glittering throng around.

"Rip Van Winkle!" exploded Voltaire. He looked wildly around him. *"Mon dieu!"* he cried. "Is it possible? Is it possible that I am forgotten?" He turned to Tom. "Look closely, young man," he said. "Don't you know me?"

"Well . . . er . . ." said Tom, "your face is kind of familiar. Can you give me a hint?"

"A hint?" said Voltaire. "Surely I have to say but one word and you will immediately know me. Eh bien! *Zaïre.*"

"*Zaïre?*" cried Tom, utterly at sea.

"*Zaïre. Irene. Mérope. Candide.* Well, you buffoon. Who am I?"

"I don't know, sir," said Tom. "Pretty names, though."

"Pretty names?" cried Voltaire. "Is it possible that you've spent your whole life among Hottentots? *Tonnerre.* Those are plays. Tremendous plays. Magnificent plays. The world's best plays—except *Candide,* which is, of course, a romance.

"Let me tell you, you poor youth who was condemned to an upbringing among savages, that *Zaïre, Irene,* and *Mérope* are better plays even than those written by Mr. Shakespeare, who was handicapped in that he had to write in English. They are better plays than those of Racine or of Molière, of whom, educated among savages, you have heard nothing. And these excellent plays, these glittering productions, were written by me. In short, sir, I am a playwright. And I am the only playwright worth remembering. I am"—he paused like one about to fling open a curtain upon the whole world—"I am Voltaire." And then in the silence that followed this earth-shaking revelation, he said, almost as an aside, "And this is an angel."

Tom, turning to Cecile, said immediately, "Oh, I knew she was an angel the moment I saw her."

"You did?" cried Voltaire. He produced a quizzing glass which hung from an austere thin black ribbon around his neck and walked around Cecile, examining her in detail with particular attention to her ankles.

"Yes," repeated Tom, "I did." At that moment the orchestra commenced to play. It was not an orchestra of the modern sort, but a very large string ensemble such as Mozart or old Haydn might have directed, and the delicate and stately lilt of a minuet came clearly to them.

Tom held out a hand to Cecile and said, "Shall we?"

"I'd love to," said Cecile, and off she went with the handsome Pennsylvania militiaman, leaving Voltaire to stare after them amazed.

"This is a farce," he said. "A farce, and in dubious taste. I, Voltaire, steal an angel from Heaven, and I am not on Earth with her two minutes before she is snapped up by a Hottentot . . ."

The crowd had thinned a little as couples moved off to the ballroom, and Jennie Truesdale, the Social Secretary, herself dressed in a hoopskirt and tiny bodice spotted Voltaire and came up to him. "Excuse me, sir," she said, "I saw you talking—but haven't I seen you somewhere before?"

"Mam'selle," said Voltaire, "before you say another word, let me assure you I am not Rip Van Winkle."

"Of course not," said Jennie. "Only a Hottentot would make a mistake like that. You are Voltaire."

"And you," said Voltaire irradiating charm on the moment, "you, whose intelligence is exceeded only by your beauty, are an angel."

"Oh, I'm not really an angel," said Jennie.

"That is a great relief to me, mam'selle, I assure you," said Voltaire. "I have found them, at times, a trifle restricting. But do not tell me who you are, for I am sure we have met before, and I also know you. You will see that I have an excellent memory. You are Émile, the Marquise de Chatelet."

"No," said Jennie, "I am not."

"How could I make such a mistake?" said Voltaire. "Of course! You are Pimpette, the charming little Protestant girl I met at The Hague."

"Alas," said Jennie with a smile, "I am not Pimpette."

"Ah," said Voltaire. "Denise . . . my dear Denise."

56

This time Jennie was a little irritated. "No," she said, "I am not Denise."

"Pompadour," said Voltaire. "Who else? But you look so much younger, *chérie* . . ."

"I am not Pompadour," said Jennie.

"Mon dieu," exclaimed Voltaire, "time plays the devil with a man's memory. I assure you, mam'selle, it was not always so. Once I could distinctly remember a lady's face for . . . well . . . at least for a year. But I am intrigued. Do not tell me your name. Permit me, mam'selle—the eyes, dazzled by beauty, must summon the hands to their aid." He closed his eyes and, placing his hands on her shoulders, ran them delicately down her arms, and then placed them on her waist . . .

"How ridiculous of me," he cried. "I could never forget that waist. You are none other than Marie, Duchesse de Maine."

"I'm not. And I think you're bragging," said Jennie.

But Voltaire was not to be discouraged. "The waist is that of Marie, Duchesse de Maine," he said. "Of that there is not the slightest doubt. But, mam'selle, there is one other aspect which reveals identity without fail. Would you be so good as to raise the hem of your dress just an inch or two so I may see your ankles?"

Jennie, annoyed and yet a little amused, did so, and Voltaire walked around her, examining her ankles through his glass with a great show of grace and expertise.

"Sufficient, mam'selle," when he had made his circuit. "I know every pair of ankles worth knowing in France, and you are not French. You are not indeed English either, for their ankles are thick, except among the de Winters, who are of French extraction. It seems that we are strangers, mam'selle. I am desolated that we have not met before."

"You seem to be doing all right for a stranger," said Jennie. "I am Jennie Truesdale, Social Secretary to the President."

Voltaire gave her a deep bow, his hand almost sweeping the floor. "Your servant, mam'selle," he said.

"Thank you," said Jennie. "You do that very nicely. You are a strange man, but I was looking for a friend . . ."

"Ah mam'selle," said Voltaire, "you have found a friend—a staunch and constant friend who will be generous and loving and true for—well, for a reasonable length of time."

"The friend I am looking for was dressed as a Pennsylvania militiaman, and I think I saw you talking to him."

"I know him well," said Voltaire. "A barbarian. He went off with an angel."

"He did?" said Jennie.

"Yes," replied Voltaire. "I also am astonished, for given the choice between yourself and an angel . . ."

"Yes . . . ?"

"As you see, mam'selle, I am still here."

"Hoping, I suppose," said Jennie, "to add another name to your half-remembered list?"

"Ah, mam'selle, do not judge so harshly," said Voltaire. "Each name is not a trophy, but a wound; a wound which through the years cries out of happiness lost. Émile, Denise, Pimpette—each name awakens a cry of pain in the heart which is never gone."

"Why so many?" said Jennie, who, born in Vermont, had had a solid, sensible, New England upbringing.

"It is a great puzzle," replied Voltaire. "Why not, indeed, just one? I have thought about it often and this is my conclusion. Each man is born incomplete. He seeks, through life, the lost part of himself. Some give up the search and die, maimed. Some are lucky and find right away what they seek. Others must search on and on, thinking that by some sunlit wall, or at the foot of a cascade of noble stairs, or in the shadow of the elms by Notre Dame, or in some sunny meadow drenched with dew, they will find that which is lost of themselves."

"And what if what is lost is never found?" asked Jennie softly.

"Out of that," said Voltaire, "come all the great works of art—the 'Pieta' of Michelangelo, da Vinci's 'Mona Lisa,' Dante's Beatrice—and my own poetry."

"I didn't think you had written any poetry," said Jennie.

"It is perhaps not well known," said Voltaire. "A play is a landscape, thrown open to thousands; a poem is a flower given to one. In any case, I had to waste a lot of my time—and of my talent—scrubbing up the verses of that egomaniac Frederick of Prussia. He had no ear for words nor any secret recesses in his heart from which to draw immortality. He thought that all that was required to write poetry was to strew French phrases around Greek goddesses like garlands, though in his case, more like weeds. What a man! He played flute like a pig suffering from asthma. His only brilliance lay in the bullying and slaughter of his fellows, and to give himself some patina of true glory he gathered in his court the best minds of Europe. It was a gross error, for he had a court of philosophers of whom he was not king but jester."

"You know," said Jennie. "Listening to you talk, I begin to think that you really are Voltaire."

To this he replied earnestly, "Mam'selle, I assure you that there is only one work of God called Voltaire, and I am he."

But Vermont is not to be swept aside by either charm or fancy, and Jennie replied, "Well, it's amusing to pretend and that's what this whole thing is about—everybody pretending to be someone else, and recalling days that are long gone. Just before I met you, I saw George the Third. And Thomas Jefferson. They were talking together."

"Where did you see them?" asked Voltaire, who had drifted off with the angel Cecile from his companions.

"Over there," said Jennie pointing. "Somewhere in that mob."

"I should find him, I suppose," said Voltaire. "We came together."

"In the same car?"

"In the same—er—vehicle," replied Voltaire.

"Vehicle," said Jennie. "What are you hiding? You surely didn't come here in a coach, drawn by horses? That would be carrying the thing too far."

Voltaire did not reply immediately. Instead he reflected on this pretty American girl who had the waist of Marie, Duchesse de Maine, and ankles of her own. She was a touch, a trifle, disappointing. There was something about her mind, some heaviness, some overpracticality which prevented her being the captivating and entrancing creature she could be.

"No, mam'selle," he said a trifle coldly. "We did not come in a coach. Arriving as we did from another time, we came in a suitable vehicle. A clock."

"A clock?" cried Jennie. "Did you say a clock?" She seemed alarmed.

"Yes," said Voltaire. "A clock. A grandfather clock. You see," he continued airily, "to gain access to places which are otherwise denied, one has to have a suitable vehicle. Often, that is all that is needed. And in this instance, our vehicle was a clock."

"Oh my gosh," said Jennie. "You used a grandfather clock . . . ?"

"Precisely," said Voltaire. "A strange entourage, I assure you. It was amusing, you must agree. Myself, King of Wit; George Washington, King of Sense; and George the Third—er—King of England."

"Who else?" said Jennie.

"Jefferson and of course the angel Cecile, who however has gone off with your young man."

"Oh my gosh," said Jennie again. "Of course she has. What else?" and off she dashed leaving Voltaire staring after her utterly astonished.

Chapter Nine

George III was stubborn but he was also a gentleman. He was perhaps the first monarch of his nation who could not understand why Englishmen should ever want to be anything else but Englishmen or—since England in his time included as satellites Scotland, Ireland, Wales, and the thirteen American colonies—British. Strolling around in the White House among the President's guests, seeing such a vast throng of happy and plainly wealthy people, seeing the deference paid to the new nation by representatives of other powers, he still thought the rebellion wrong. It had violated a fundamental principle. That principle was that all should glory in the name of Britain and equally that nations should be ruled by kings who alone could unite all the parties and be a true father to the national family.

His queen, Charlotte, was pleased with the excitement of the ball; the beautifully dressed crowd, the amazing lights; the music, the laughter, and the talk. She was a plain dull nice woman with a plain dull nice mind, and she said to the King that matters must have turned out well in America because everybody was happy, and it seemed that the country had now lasted two hundred years. (They had soon discovered that the reason for the ball was to celebrate the bicentennial of Independence.)

"Bah," said the King, lowering himself into a chair, for his feet hurt from strolling about. "Mere duration, madam, is no test of worth. Hell itself has lasted since Lucifer's revolt and on your principle Hell could be said to be highly successful. A fig for duration. It is by other measures that the matter must be assayed."

"But, sir," said the Queen, "see how happy everyone is— it is like a country wedding in the old days."

"Happiness is no test of merit either, madam," replied her spouse. "I recall the wording of that Declaration which brought this revolt to a head. It contained one phrase which damned the whole document. 'Life, liberty and the pursuit of happiness.' There is a snare for fools, madam, for if everyone seeks his own happiness what is to become of Society?

"Duty is man's first obligation—duty to God, duty to his King, duty to his nation, and duty to his neighbor. Unless that principle is universally acknowledged nothing but chaos can result. You may distrust as a blackguard any man who, seeking power, promises you happiness. True happiness can come only from duty done. It is not in the gift of politicians.

"Besides," he continued, looking about for a servant to remove his shoe and massage his foot, "this is a poor place to come to see how a nation fares. Would you go to Vauxhall Gardens on May Day to judge the state of England?"

"No," said the Queen.

"We should be talking to some farmer over a gate," said the King. "Not sitting in a palace surrounded by popinjays. Hey, fellow. Put that tray down and take off my shoe." (This to a waiter passing by with a tray of drinks.) But the waiter went on, and when two or three others, hailed in the same manner, did likewise, the King bent over to remove his shoe himself. But at this point a man who had been watching the two for a while came over and saying, "Allow me, your Majesty," dropped to one knee and removed the shoe.

"Much obliged," said the King. "Damned civil of you, I

62

must say. Servants, as usual, are all deaf in the presence of their masters. Who are you?"

The man, dressed in the modest homespun of a Quaker, produced from his waistcoat pocket a visiting card which he presented to the King. The King, holding it at arm's length, for he hated to wear glasses, read aloud the words:

Elroyd P. Simpkins
FOOT SPECIALIST

"You're British, aren't you?" said Mr. Simpkins when the King had read the card and handed it with a grunt to his queen.

"Born and bred, and glory in the name," said the King.

"The British are very popular here now," said Mr. Simpkins. "Henry the Eighth and Queen Elizabeth and all that stuff from the BBC, you know. And before that, the Beatles. Quite a conquest."

The King was immediately interested. "What's that?" he said. "What's that? Conquest, did you say?"

"Sure," said the man. "I tell you they've just about swept the nation. It's that British accent—that's the in-thing. I remember when if you spoke with a Limey accent about all you'd get out of it was a black eye. Now, we have English radio announcers and television announcers and everything. I'll bet you'd be a knockout on television. Sweep the country."

"That wasn't my impression at our last acquaintance," said the King, interested nonetheless.

"Oh, but you are wrong," said Mr. Simpkins. "Why, on television—just doing a little commercial—nothing in poor taste, you know—you'd soon be better known and more popular even perhaps than the President."

"What do you mean—television?" cried the King.

"Why, you know—just a little spot and then your picture

would be shown in every household in the nation. We could fix it right now. You're dressed perfectly for the part. You see that cameraman there?" He pointed to a man with a television camera held by a shoulder support like a gun. "That cameraman there has shot about half the commercial already. You reaching down to take off your shoe and me coming over and doing it for you and rubbing your foot. Now, all we have to do is for me to spray your foot, right through the sock, with this"—he produced a small spray can—"and then you say into the mike"—he produced a microphone—"'Simpkins Soothing Spray—there's a kingdom of comfort in it.' And then you hold this little thing up in front of you."

"Tell me again," said the King. "How do you get my picture into every household in this nation?"

"Television—like I told you," said Mr. Simpkins and pointed again to the cameraman.

"That's something quite new to us," said the Queen.

"You play the part real well," said Mr. Simpkins. "You really do. Well, is it agreed? Remember, you just say into this, 'Simpkins Soothing Spray—there's a kingdom of comfort in it.' And you hold up the can."

The King wasn't sure what he was doing, but the thought of his picture being in the home of everybody in America was enough of a spur, and the price to be paid for this tremendous achievement seemed minuscule—a sentence of pure balderdash which as far as he was concerned would be heard only by those around him. So he agreed.

Mr. Simpkins sprayed his foot to his instant relief, and the cameraman was able to record that relief in a closeup of the King's face. Then the King said (for he had always had an excellent memory), "Simpkins Soothing Spray—there's a kingdom of comfort in it," and held up the container.

The whole scene took but a moment and then Mr. Simpkins gave the King a paper to sign, which the King signed, for part of his function was signing things. Mr. Simpkins said that it was a release which permitted him to show the King's picture throughout the United States, and Mr. Simpkins then put his shoe back on for him and told him to keep the can of foot spray. He added, "You have a good television presence, sir; and I have no doubt that if you were a citizen, you could achieve high office, even the Presidency, by just remembering to keep the best side of your face toward the camera—and looking reliable—which means not too clever."

"There," said the King, turning to his Queen. "I knew that they really loved me. It was that damned upstart Washington and that confounded Congress that always stood between me and my people. My picture in every home, and the British more popular here than ever before. That's what he said. Wait until Washington hears about that." He looked about him now with enormous satisfaction.

"I should judge, madam," he continued, "from what I see before me, that the nation is in a condition of greatest prosperity. The national income may well be in excess of a hundred million sterling a year. Yes, a hundred million sterling. The tax on tea I now admit was a mistake and probably couldn't be renewed. But there are without a doubt other articles of trade. . . ." His eye fell upon the spray can. "A tax on something such as this, widely used, at the rate of a penny or two, would without a doubt raise an ample revenue . . ."

The King was interrupted by yet another guest who plumped himself down in a nearby chair and, glancing first at the King and then at the Queen, said without further introduction, "Say, you two look like the real thing. Better than Hollywood. Every time Hollywood puts on something like this, you can see the phony sticking out a mile. I saw a movie once where they had this gladiator with a Bronx accent fighting with a lion that came from New Jersey. I laughed fit to burst. I'll bet you're British."

"Indeed I am, sir," said the King, not a little pleased that

65

this seemed evident to everyone, for in his own lifetime he had had to fight against accusations of being German.

"Okay," said the man. "Now I want to ask you a question. What do you think of this whole thing? I mean the United States. We started off fighting you. Now here we are. Now what do you think of it?"

"Sir," said the King. "I will tell you very plainly . . ."

But his queen cut him off. "We have very little acquaintance with this country," she said. "And have really come here to find out something about it. We can hardly say what we think of it until we know something of its condition."

"Now there's a switch for you," said the other. "If you were one of us I expect you'd have told me everything that was the matter with the country whether you knew anything about it or not. I mean we're the world experts on everything —Korea, Vietnam, Cambodia, Israel, Egypt, Syria, Lebanon— you name it and we've got the solution. Only thing is that none of the solutions ever stick and smart as we are we never see a problem until the thing blows up in our face.

"Now you take that war. There we were throwing away billions of gallons of oil a month bombing people who never heard of us and all the time those know-it-alls didn't know we were headed into a worldwide oil shortage. A world oil shortage, mind you, and they're still throwing the stuff away like it was water . . ."

The rest of what he said was utterly lost on both the King and the Queen. The King, after a while, decided the man was a professional discontent and very probably a Whig for he had the pasty face of a Whig, and an expression of both piety and patience which, to the King, was the very stamp of treason. However when the man started talking about taxation, the King picked up his ears.

"Now just think of it," he said. " 'No taxation without representation'—that was what the whole gimmick was about. And we pretty soon learned that the reverse was true—no

66

Representation without Taxation. The more representation you get, the more taxes you have to pay. All you got to do is elect a new body to do something and the next thing you know, they're taxing you for something—for your own good, of course. City taxes, county taxes, water district taxes, school district taxes, hospital district taxes, sales taxes, real estate taxes, federal taxes. You name it, they got it. We'd have been better off under the King, if you ask me. Well, nice talking to you. See you," and off he went as suddenly as he had appeared.

" 'Better off under the King,' " said George III. "There you have it, my dear. They made a mistake, and now they know it. Wait until I find that fellow Jefferson and Washington. My picture to be in every house in the nation and strangers admitting they would have been better off if they'd remained British."

"I don't like that man," said the Queen quietly. "When someone comes up to a perfect stranger and starts denouncing his own country right away, there's usually something the matter with the man, and not with the country. Had he been British, he would have been denouncing us to the Americans. Of that I'm sure. I don't sense any widespread discontent. The people all seem very happy to me. And as for an oil shortage, wherever could he get that idea? There must be a thousand lights around here and everyone of them burning briskly."

"I found the fellow very honest," grunted the King.

"Sir," said the Queen, "it is surely a mistake to confuse agreement with honesty, and it is often the mark of an honest man that he quarrels with you."

"When a man quarrels with me," said the King, "it is nothing else but the mark of a quarrelsome man."

Chapter Ten

Jefferson was greatly taken with the White House, on which a considerable amount of work had been done by the start of his first term, so that he was the first President to have occupied it. He had shared the building then, during the daytime hours, with plasterers, builders, bricklayers, stonemasons, carpenters, and plumbers; and indeed he had had to wait a few months before he could move in from his lodgings in Canaird's boardinghouse while sufficient rooms were prepared for his use. At Canaird's he had had dinner at the common table with the other lodgers, refusing even to sit at the head for, as he explained, he was the President of a Republic, not the sovereign of a nation. But when he moved at last into the White House, he often dined alone, for he was a widower, and he didn't believe in lavish entertainments or standing upon ceremony, an attitude which irritated the socially conscious citizens of the muddy little village called Washington, D.C.

"What a difference," he exclaimed to Washington when the two of them, accompanied by Martha Washington, had managed to struggle out of the building to get a general view of it from the grounds. "In my time the roof leaked atrociously, for there were not enough slates for tiling, there were no storehouses or washhouses and not even a stable for the horses. I had to stable my horses in rented premises a quarter of a mile away; and when I wanted to take a ride on Wildair (splendid hunter—you remember Wildair?) it was an hour before he could be saddled and brought around to me. No plastering at all had been done in the eastern part of the building, and all the furniture was second or third hand. Good enough, though. I particularly liked the scarlet plush that I inherited from your days and used in the main withdrawing room. I never could see, in any case, why a President should fare better than the average of the people over whose nation they have called on him to preside."

Washington grunted. "Never wanted the office myself," he said shortly. "My view was that if they wanted me to be President it would have to be at my level of living and nobody else's. I was never a snob, I trust, but I hope always a gentleman. I saw no reason to lower my standards in order to be President. Well, Tom. You admire the building. I'm off to talk to whoever I can. We've been here only five minutes, I suppose, but it certainly seems to me that our revolution was an outstanding success."

Off he went without another word, leaving Jefferson in raptures over the floodlit White House, the East Terrace he had fought so hard to preserve, the carefully placed and huge windows and the Grecian grace of the whole structure. Before he died, the White House had been largely finished, though the British had burned it in part in the War of 1812, of which he had but the dimmest memories. Yet here it was, two hundred years later, and as lovely a building as a lovely land could hope for.

The lawn on which he now stood taking in the prospect had in his day been a wilderness in which Lewis and Clark, returning from their expedition, had turned loose several bears they had brought back with them as presents. It had been said then that the President lived in a bear garden. He didn't mind at all, for he had a great love for animals.

"Hey," said a voice beside him, "you look more like Mr. Jefferson than anything I ever saw including his portrait. You

69

must be an actor too." Jefferson turned and was surprised to see a black man and his wife standing beside him, dressed in what he took to be modern dress.

"Why," said Jefferson, "you have the advantage of me. You know my name but I have not the honor of your acquaintance."

"You kidding?" said the black man. "Take a close look. You trying to say you don't know me?"

"I'm sorry," said Jefferson. "I don't want to offend you, but I do not know you. I've—er—been away a long time and in a very distant part and only just arrived back in this country." He hesitated. "You are a freed man?" he asked.

"It's getting that way," said the other. "You're not jiving, are you?"

"I'm telling the truth," said Jefferson, who wasn't at all sure of the meaning of the word *jive*.

"My name's Harris," said the man. "Robert Harris. Which you probably know anyway, because I'm a movie and TV star and used to be a baseball player, and I'm an activist in the Black Liberation Movement."

"The blacks are not free *yet?*" asked Jefferson as if this news rent his heart.

"Well, we can vote now," said Mr. Harris. "That took two wars—one called the Civil War and the other they haven't put a name on it yet. It also took four or five world heavyweight champions, maybe twenty good ballplayers, a bunch of maybe-good-guys-turned-killers, and a lot of riots. You never heard of any of those things?"

"Never," said Jefferson.

Mr. Harris turned to his wife. "You know," he said, "this cat is one hell of an actor. He could play the part in any movie the British Broadcasting Corporation made to celebrate the bicentennial."

"He could play the part in any movie made over here to celebrate the bicentennial," said his wife.

70

"Uh, uh," said Mr. Harris. "You've never read those scripts." He eyed Jefferson closely. "You an actor too?" he asked.

"No," said Jefferson. "I'm a—a farmer, mostly; an estate owner, driven into politics by the pressure of the times. Or rather—I was."

This plainly was not believed, and Jefferson considered the problem for the moment. Then he said, "Since you say you are an actor yourself, Mr. Harris, perhaps you could amuse yourself, while we rest on the bench here, by pretending that *I* am Thomas Jefferson—the real Thomas Jefferson —returned to Earth, and you are trying to explain to me the progress your people—slaves for the greater part in my time— have made in this country since my death."

"Starting in like you knew nothing whatever about it?"

"Starting in with the fact that when I drafted the Declaration of Independence I denounced slavery, but that was stricken from the Declaration by the Congress, and when I died I freed those of my slaves who had a trade and could support themselves, and gave them enough money in my will to get them started in business."

"You did?" said Mr. Harris.

"Yes," said Jefferson. "It was little enough. Many others did as much. But these were little things that did nothing to solve the whole wretched problem."

Mr. Harris then related all he knew, and it was a great deal, of the efforts of black Americans to rise from slavery to acceptance as citizens, and added that many prominent blacks, in disgust with Christianity, which had permitted slavery, had become Mohammedans.

"Strange," said Jefferson, "strange indeed. While I ever maintained that a man's religious beliefs are his own business, I do not see that much is to be gained by changing from one sect which purchased slaves to another sect which sold them."

The other ignored this. "I want to ask you a few questions," he said. "Going along with the gag that you are Thomas Jefferson."

"I will answer to the best of my ability," replied Jefferson.

"Why didn't you free the blacks at the start of the revolution?" demanded Harris.

"I suppose you would not believe me if I said it was because they would have starved to death or suffered dreadful privations for lack of food, shelter, or employment if free," said Jefferson quietly.

"I've heard that so often it makes me sick," said Mr. Harris.

"I heard it so often it made me sick," said Jefferson. "Yet to a degree it was true, though it was not the whole answer. The whole answer was this: Our people at that time were not sufficiently devoted to freedom for themselves to free others."

"That I don't dig at all," said Mr. Harris.

"Sir," said Jefferson rising, "the man who owns a slave, or lives by exploiting others, whether slave or not, is not himself a free man. He is a man who must look over his shoulder all the time, in fear. True freedom lies in a deep concern for the freedom of others, and if this is accepted it should make every man, out of pure selfishness, the ardent devotee of the freedom of his neighbor." With that, he rose, bowed to the two of them, and withdrew.

"That's a real smooth cat," said Mr. Harris. "Let's go see if there's any of that ice cream torte left."

Washington, meanwhile, strolling around the grounds and glad to get out of the press of people within the White House, was several times offended by some who called after him, "Hi, George." His nature had always been to stand on ceremony, and even with his closest friends, he had always avoided familiarity. When he himself had entertained at the Presidential residence in Philadelphia (for he had never occupied the White House as President) he had been at a loss as to how to retain his dignity and at the same time not offend people. He solved the problem by sitting, during his levees

72

and social occasions, on a small dais at the end of the room, where with his wife he could nod his head to all who nodded their heads to him.

Even so he was aware that he made enemies and once burst out to Jefferson, "By God, sir, some of them complain that I don't nod as warmly to them as I nod to someone else. There's no pleasing such a pack. My face gets sore from smiling and my confounded teeth keep working loose." (They had never fitted, though Revere and others had worked them over time and time again.)

To this Jefferson had mildly counseled that he move about among his guests instead of sitting above them and greet them all with affability. But Washington's training (other than that of gentleman farmer) was all that of a soldier, and military discipline and affability do not go together.

Thus, in moving about the White House grounds, he ignored the shouts of "Hi, George" which the rabble in Philadelphia and New York had often sent after him in his time on Earth, and looked about for a man of equal station—which he could judge only from his dress. His wife, seeing her good friend Queen Charlotte quite alone, begged leave to go about with her, promising they would return to the front hall of the White House in an hour where they could easily be found. Washington, alone, came at length upon a gentleman dressed as a colonel of the Pennsylvania Line and, recognizing the uniform, was moved to talk to him without introduction.

"Good evening, sir," he said. "A pleasant occasion, I think. And at prosperous times for the nation."

"Prosperous?" said the other. "Why, in six months there's going to be a breadline around the block like in Hoover's day. The dollar is worth thirty percent less in purchasing power than ten years ago, costs are rising every day, and the President is running the country as if he were the patrol leader and we were all Boy Scouts."

73

"I gather you are of the opposing party," said Washington smoothly. "What in your view is the principal source of trouble?"

"Nobody knows," said the other. "Maybe it's the Japanese selling everything over here they can, from automobiles to guitars, at prices we can't afford to make them at. Maybe it's the switch from a war-oriented economy to a peace-oriented economy. Maybe it's because nobody in government has any brains though it can't be that, because nobody in government ever has had any brains. Maybe it's because this is an election year. But whatever it is, we're out of ideas and words too. Recession, depression, cost crisis, material shortage, production imbalance, distribution malfunction—I've heard them all. We've run out of words for the cure too. We've tried New Deal, New Frontier, Affluent Society, War on Poverty, War on Plenty, and now, like I say, we're going through the *Boy Scout Handbook* in case there's something we overlooked there. Maybe we have. But I see nothing ahead but disaster."

"No real change," said Washington happily. "No real change at all. Food high, I suppose?"

"Out of sight."

"Money depreciated in value?"

"Yes."

"Army too expensive and should be cut drastically?"

"Yes."

"Same for the Navy?"

"Yes."

"Farmers unable to secure reasonable prices for their crops?"

"Right."

"Strange," said Washington. He looked about not only at the sumptuous White House and the glittering grounds, but at the lights of the vast city beyond the railings which was named after him. "Strange," he repeated. "Strange how one disaster after another through two hundred years should

74

have led to the tremendous improvements I see around me."

"I don't know about the last two hundred years," said the other, "but if something isn't done to restore the value of wages in the next two hundred days, there's going to be some rioting about this place."

"I don't doubt it," said Washington. "It was exactly the same in my day. Apprentice riots, workingmen's riots, Shay's Rebellion over the whiskey tax. And yet, all in all, the nation survived and, all in all, decade by decade, prospered. I think the solution lies in this: that men are more ingenious than the difficulties they face and that a day, a week, or a year is too short a span in which to judge the conditions of things. We are usually better than we think we are. Well, sir, I give you good day." Off he went then, leaving the colonel of the Pennsylvania Line (who was actually the president of one of the great labor unions) to stare after him.

"What a nut," he said at length. "You can't judge how things are in one day. You have to wait ten years. Well, I don't hurt over ten years, or a hundred for that matter. I hurt in one day. Must be a college teacher. Wouldn't make a President. Never. No grasp."

Chapter Eleven

Shortly after these initial encounters with their countrymen of two hundred years later, both Jefferson and Washington were arrested, fingerprinted, and mugged by the White House police. They were charged with trespassing in the White House, invasion of federal property, resisting arrest, and refusing to reveal their identities to authorized persons.

The arrest was the result of Jennie Truesdale's talk with Voltaire. Voltaire had mentioned quite casually that they had all got into the White House with a clock, and Jennie, with bomb threats ever in the back of her mind since the clock's disappearance, had rushed off to find Tom Czeuleger with the news that several men, in disguise, were at that moment in the White House with the missing grandfather clock.

Tom, at the time, was dancing a minuet with the angel Cecile, who called him "dear brother" in the most entrancing tones. But on getting this news he left immediately, leaving Cecile on the dance floor.

Tom found Washington and Jefferson on the stairs leading to the President's study on an upper floor and asked them to come with him. He took them to his office and asked for their identification—driver's licenses, Social Security cards, credit cards—and the invitation to the celebration. Of course they had none of these things and didn't know what they were, and Washington got a little heated and said that when a gentleman gave his name, no other gentleman would question it. Matters were not helped in the slightest by the two insisting they came from Heaven. So Tom handed them over to the White House police, who booked and fingerprinted and photographed them. Tom then called Ted Storhill of Security Headquarters, to alert him that the missing clock was somewhere in the White House and had been brought in by a group of men costumed as Washington, Jefferson, George III, and Voltaire—with two lady accomplices.

Storhill asked Tom whether the two in custody claimed to belong to any liberation group. "They say they come from Heaven," said Tom, "and that they are devoted to life, liberty and the pursuit of happiness."

"Sounds like those Symbionese nuts," said Storhill. "Any weapons?"

"None."

"Do they belong to an underprivileged group?"

"Well, they're all White Anglo-Saxon Protestants," said Tom.

"Don't get smart with me," snarled Storhill. "You know what I mean. Where do they come from?"

"I just told you—Heaven. They gave some rigmarole about a discussion, at what they call The Club in Heaven, about whether the American Revolution was a success, and they came here to find out."

"That's it," said Storhill. "All these activists start out by questioning the Revolution. Book them for everything you can think of, and meanwhile I'll get busy picking up the others and looking for that clock. The clock's the important thing. It's bound to be a bomb. But it shouldn't be hard to find—if we have time."

Voltaire was the next to be picked up, and when he also was booked and photographed and fingerprinted, he turned to the others and said, "What a compliment! They still recognize me as a philosopher."

"What has being a philosopher got to do with the present situation?" asked Jefferson.

"My good sir," said Voltaire, "philosophers, in the traditions of the Old World are all either imprisoned or put to death, as you may discover if you will reflect on the list from, say, Socrates to Bertrand Russell. In my own time on Earth, I had to flee both France and Germany to avoid one fate or the other. Now here I am imprisoned again. It's encouraging, I assure you, particularly since the man responsible for my arrest first thought I was Rip Van Winkle."

He was very happy about the whole matter. "What I have said about what is done to philosophers," he continued, "applies only to Western civilization. In the West, governments persecute thinkers, recognizing the danger of any kind of philosophical thought. In the East, on the other hand, thinkers are revered, and no one would ever have thought of imprisoning or putting to death Buddha or Confucius."

All the photographing and fingerprinting and questioning had done nothing whatever, of course, to uncover a conspiracy among them aimed at the President, or shake their claimed identity. It didn't even help to establish their identity. There were no fingerprints anywhere on record to match theirs, nor photographs either, though Tom had to admit that Washington and Jefferson bore a resemblance to their own likenesses on postage stamps.

Questioned about the clock, they said it was merely an essential vehicle and were outraged to discover that Tom and the Security Police believed that the clock was a bomb, intended to kill the President and many of his guests.

"Good heavens, sir," cried Washington, "we pledged our lives, our fortunes, and our honor to establish this country. Why, if there were any threat to the person of the man who is President now, I would die to defend him."

"An excellent sentiment," said Voltaire. "But, alas, you are already dead."

78

"We could clear up this whole thing if you'd tell me just where that clock is," said Tom.

But they couldn't tell him. They had entered the clock in the reading room of The Club and found themselves immediately in the White House and in the twentieth century.

This impasse might have continued indefinitely had it not been for the angel Cecile. Tom had left her on the ballroom floor. She was, of course, not the only angel there. Everyone in that crowded ballroom, heads of state, cabinet ministers, envoys of every rank, industrialists and labor leaders, civil servants and guests of every race, political view, and religious belief had each his or her own guardian angel. So there was a host of angels on the ballroom floor watching over their human charges—some with a look of deep concern on their faces.

While the President's guests danced the minuet, their angelic guardians floated about among them, singing hosannas to the greater glory of God and undulating at the same time in a sort of hula dance, though of a more spiritual cast. Only one human present was aware of their presence—an ancient priest of the Dominican Order who, as the oldest native-born cleric in the United States, was a guest at the celebration. He sat smiling in a corner, one venerable foot tapping to the beat of the minuet and a smile on his face as he watched the angels and listened to their praises of God. Those who passed him by, seeing him smiling and looking vaguely and delightedly upward, thought him senile.

Cecile, who had been distracted by the handsome young American in the uniform of the Pennsylvania militia with whom she had been dancing, now remembered her charges. They were none of them to be seen.

"Where is the English saint known as George the Third?" she asked one of her sister angels and was told instantly that George III was at that moment in the office of the President of the United States.

79

Cecile flew there instantly and found the King, red-faced, insisting that he was indeed George III, and the President, white-faced, seated in an easy chair, and fearful of assassination, glancing toward a distant telephone, convinced he was in the presence of a madman.

"George the Third," repeated the King. "Plain as a pikestaff. Can't you even make an effort to believe me, sir? Is your mind to be closed to everything that has the slightest aspect of novelty?"

"Calm yourself," said the President. "Calm yourself. I do believe you. I assure you I believe you."

The President's guardian angel shook her head, very worried. "It's a great big fib," she said to Cecile. "He's fallen into a habit of fibs. It's been getting worse and worse ever since he was elected."

"What Saint George the Third says is true," Cecile assured her. "Your ward will be in no spiritual danger whatever in believing him. You should influence his mind to accept it."

"I don't like to interfere," said the President's guardian angel. "I'm really just supposed to watch and record and guard when I can. But not interfere with his will."

"I think you are supposed to dispose the mind of your charge to acceptance of grace and truth. Isn't that so, dear sister?" asked Cecile.

The President's angel looked dubiously at the stocky and irate figure of George III. "*He* doesn't look much like grace and truth," she said.

"He's a saint," replied Cecile, "and, dear sister, you should predispose the mind of your charge to believe in the saints."

There could be no argument, moral, spiritual, metaphysical, or theological against this statement, and so the President's guardian angel slipped a finger between the alpha, beta, gamma, delta, epsilon, and other waves given out in whirls, circles, parallelograms, and equilateral triangles by the President's brain and in so doing set up such a vibration that the President instantly believed beyond any quibble of doubt that it was indeed George III who stood before him.

Indeed, he could not understand for a moment how he could have doubted the truth of so obvious a fact and, getting up quickly, he moved toward the King and said, "Please, please forgive me. I have been dealing with so many experts and authorities on one subject and another recently that I have developed a habit of believing nothing. I thought you an imbecile, or an expert, and it is quite difficult to see the difference between the two of them at times. Ridiculous, isn't it, that I can accept the existence of quarks and mesons, neutrons, antineutrons and atomic particles so minute that they can, I am assured, penetrate a million miles of solid lead without leaving a trace; and yet doubt the existence of spirits and angels who can do precisely the same thing. Indeed now that I place the two side by side—quarks and spirits as it were— it seems to me that the overwhelming weight of both human evidence through centuries and plain sense lies strongly on the side of spirits. . . ."

He was about to continue in this vein when the telephone rang. He excused himself and answered it. Storhill was on the line. Much of what Storhill said initially made little sense to the President. But out of his disconnected and jumbled report the President gathered that the White House was being searched for a grandfather clock containing a bomb, and it might be necessary to evacuate the whole building right in the middle of the Presidential Ball. The clock, it seemed, had been smuggled into the White House by members of some kind of "liberation army" disguised as eminent persons who had mingled with the guests.

"We've got three of them here, Chief," said Storhill. "Washington, Jefferson, and Voltaire—that's what they call themselves. We're looking for the clock and three others— George the Third, his Queen, and another female dressed as Washington's wife . . ."

81

"Storhill," said the President, cutting him off, "you listen to me very carefully. You bring those three to my office immediately, drop your search for the clock, and say nothing about this to anybody. You understand . . . ?"

"But, Chief . . ." said Storhill.

"Do what I say," snapped the President. "It's just possible that you have managed to arrest the three most distinguished guests this nation has ever had."

"But the bomb, Chief . . ." said Storhill.

"There isn't any bomb," said the President. "For your information, George the Third is with me right now and I'm entirely satisfied with his explanation of how he got here. Bring the others and get this straight. I will hold you personally responsible for seeing that not a word of this gets to the press or anybody outside of your organization. Our nation has been presented with a magnificent and unexpected and highly secret opportunity, and I don't want it ruined by any bungling on your part."

When the President hung up, Storhill stared unbelievingly at the telephone for several moments and then dialed Tom Czeuleger's office with sudden decision.

"You goofed," he said. "You've arrested three eminent guests who came here incognito for discussions with the President. He was expecting them. Take those three gentlemen up to the President's office personally, destroy all the fingerprints and photographs and records made. And you might start thinking about what you're going to do for amuse- ment for the next twenty years on Wake Island or some place like it."

Tom, thunderstruck by this turn of events, escorted the three to the President's office. The President received them with every show of honor and affection and courtesy, seated them, and dismissed Tom. Then, returning to his desk, he sat down himself—and switched on his tape recorder.

Chapter Twelve

George III got along famously with President Williamson from the start. Within half an hour of the opening of their discussion he was the President's fervent supporter and admirer.

"Why," he cried, "you have fulfilled in your office every hope I ever had for the throne and indeed exceeded many of them brilliantly. You have the power to seize industries and operate them by the government. You have the power to send troops wherever you think it necessary; to do whatever you say is necessary. You have the power to regulate prices and wages and to negotiate secretly with other nations on issues of vital importance . . ."

"All in cases of national emergency only," said the President.

"Of course, of course," said the King. "That goes without saying. One doesn't go to war out of a personal whim—something important has to be involved—a matter of succession to a particular throne, the balance of power, problems beyond the wit and knowledge of the common people who are in any case too busy with their own affairs to be concerned with them. But between what you have made of your office and what I had hoped for mine, there is not a tittle of difference, and I congratulate you, sir, in succeeding where I, despite every effort I could make, failed."

"There is a great deal of difference," said Jefferson stiffly. "The President, whatever his powers, is elected for a prescribed term of four years. If he's not suitable he is thrown out of office at the end of that time, and his power then ceases."

"But, my dear fellow," said the King, "what a nonsensical procedure! Why, in four years a fellow could hardly be expected to learn the ins and outs of running a small drapery shop let alone how to be king—or president, as you prefer to call it—of a large nation."

"It is a better procedure than accepting as the ruler of a country someone who merely happens to have been born into a certain family called royal," snapped Jefferson, who was getting quite heated because he suspected he was wrong.

"How ignorant you are of the whole thing," said George smoothly. "I begin to understand now why we quarreled—it was the result of pure ignorance and oversimplification on your part. Now take my own case. From boyhood I was trained to be a king. 'Be a king, George,' my mother said on every occasion, 'and do try to keep from spilling jam on your clean shirt.' Why, while other young fellows were off cockfighting, bullbaiting, or flying kites, or running around the streets in gangs and having glorious times, I got lecture after lecture on history, on law, on the workings of Parliament, on the power of the great Whig and Tory families; how to bribe and how to threaten; how to reward and how to punish; how to expose and how to conceal; in short the whole business of government, so that when I took over I was thoroughly fitted to be a ruler and handle any kind of skulduggery the part required.

"Do you really insist, sir, that your candidates for President get that kind of training from boyhood? Not for a moment. Why on my way up here someone told me that the most important thing in becoming President is always to keep the best side of your face to the camera, and try to look as though you could be trusted."

84

Washington was outraged by such a view and thinking he saw a flaw in the King's argument, he pounced on it immediately. "You are overlooking the fact that in the case of a king who is a thorough scoundrel, the people, under the British system, have no means of removing him other than by revolution. We can remove a President unworthy of the office very simply by the thoroughly constitutional process of impeachment."

But at these words President Williamson blushed deeply. "That is, we *can* on paper," he said meekly.

"What do you mean *on paper?*" thundered Washington. "The process of impeachment is spelled out in the Constitution—and it is there for use."

"So it is," said the President. "But in practice, it not only doesn't work, it has proved almost a disaster to the nation. It takes so much of the time of the Congress, it calls for the expenditure of so much money, it so divides and demoralizes the nation, it so interferes with the business of government at home and abroad, it so detracts from the standing of the nation before the world, as political linen is publicly washed, it so destroys the confidence of the people in the whole government process, that the last time we tried to impeach a President, everybody breathed a sigh of relief when the President just resigned rather than face trial."

He paused and added, "That may well have been the most patriotic gesture he ever made. Of one thing I am sure. Of whatever he may be thought guilty in the future no President of the United States will ever again be impeached. Never! Impeachment, in practice, is not a method of getting rid of a President. It is rather a method of destroying the Presidency."

"The British system is in this respect entirely superior," said the King calmly. "We had one thoroughly bad king in a hundred or so, charged him with high treason, tried him by a court whose object was to save the nation, not the king, and cut off his head. The effect upon subsequent kings, myself

85

included, was thoroughly healthful, and of course there were no pensions to pay to survivors or other onerous expenses.

"But what of your Parliament?" he continued, "supposing its members are thoroughly out of step with the wishes of the people? What is the remedy?"

"You mean our Congress," said Jefferson.

"Your Congress then. If they are doing things entirely contrary to the wishes of the people, do they all have to resign?"

"Not at all," said Jefferson. "Particular members who have acted contrary to the wishes of their constituency—which, of course, is not the whole nation at all—may face the prospect of being thrown out when they come up for reelection."

"But the whole body is not required to resign if the majority party is defeated on a major issue?" demanded the King.

"Oh no," said the President. "That would leave the country without a government."

"My dear sir," said the King solemnly, "as I see it, you haven't got a government to start with. All you have is a power structure—a Congress fighting for power against a President fighting for power, with the people nowhere." A new thought now concerned him. "Of what extent is the nation at the present time?" he asked.

"Extent?" echoed President Williamson.

"How many people are there in the country?"

"In round figures, two hundred million."

"And the numbers of their representatives in Parliament?"

"In Congress," said President Williamson. "There are four hundred thirty-five in the lower house, the House of Representatives. And one hundred in the upper house, the Senate. Making a total of five hundred thirty-five in all."

"Good God," said the King. "Five hundred and thirty-five

to represent a nation of around two hundred million! That's not a democracy. It's oligarchy."

But it was Jefferson who exploded the loudest. "Five hundred and thirty-five representatives to represent two hundred million people?" he exclaimed. "We have been betrayed! The proportion is infamous—tyrannical! In round figures that means but one representative of whatever sort for every four hundred thousand citizens."

Washington exploded too. "Betrayed!" he shouted. "Betrayed! You have made a joke of our revolt, and turned men into mere ciphers, ruled by an exclusive club whose members need give no heed at all to less than half a million voices raised in protest over the same issue—if that could ever be achieved."

"There is only one way out of this whole thing," said the King firmly. "You must admit that you have made a mistake and petition the mother country to be admitted to the fold."

"You've taken leave of your senses, sir," cried Jefferson. "Admit our revolution was wrong? Never!"

"Reverse the surrender of Yorktown—impossible," cried Washington.

"Suspend the Constitution, the Bill of Rights—end the whole interminable struggle between House and Senate, White House and Supreme Court?" said the President. "Let us not be too hasty. There may be something to be said for that. Do you suppose the British would have us back?" (It must be remembered that the President was still under angelic influence to accept the proposals of King George as a saint imbued with heavenly grace.)

"Of course we would take you back, my dear fellow," said the King. "We have always had a soft spot for the underdog—for the defeated. It would be, I suppose, just a matter of abolishing the Constitution, rescinding the Declaration of

Independence, and returning to British rule. Just for a while, to be sure, until you get the hang of things and learn not to overthrow governments in petty panics and develop once again a respect for people as opposed to a respect for success and power only.

"After that," he continued, "you could become independent again, within the Commonwealth—like Canada, New Zealand, and Australia. Self-governing in every respect though spiritually united with your fellow members of the Commonwealth by the Crown. Every citizen would have his rights guaranteed by a long tradition of fair play rather than by a short Constitution which can be twisted this way and that way by clever lawyers in the course of interminable court proceedings. Come. You have a second chance. Be bold enough to seize it."

"It has merit," said the President meditatively. "The present system under which just over five hundred people pretend to represent the vital interests of some two hundred million seems to have run its course. Although we have electronic devices for vote-counting these days, which make indirect representation unnecessary, it is a fact of history that no country has ever really trusted democracy. We couldn't let our people vote directly on major issues such as peace and war, taxation, exploration of space, government-sponsored euthanasia, and so on, for the simple reason that—well—you just can't trust the people to do what you *want* them to do. Under the British system, if the majority party insists on doing what the people don't want, then the Parliament is dissolved, and that is at least a step in the direction of democracy. Yes. I must say that yours is a little more responsive and representative than ours—and yet . . ."

He paused and looked at the King, a trifle embarrassed.

"If we turned in your direction," he said, "I suppose the ranks of earl, duke, baron, baronet, knight, and dame would be available . . ."

"Of course," said the King heartily. "I should think the

first move would be to create about ten thousand knights in the next Honor's List, and then there would be the necessary heralds—blue mantle, pursuivant, portcullis, pendragon and so on . . . together with the appropriate coronets, belts, robes, ermine tippets . . ."

"That would be a great help in obtaining national acceptance for such a daring scheme," said the President. "Although we as a nation are openly and publicly devoted to the republican concept, there is nothing we dote on quite so much as nobility and rank."

Whatever he was going to say further, he was cut off by the ringing of the telephone. The President picked it up, listened, grunted a word or two, and, hanging up, said, "Gentleman, you must excuse me for a moment. I will be back in a short while. Make yourselves entirely comfortable. I am to read the Declaration of Independence on worldwide television, and when I return we can go on with your novel and attractive, indeed hopeful, suggestion."

Off he went, and a few moments later, to their astonishment, they heard his voice, seemingly coming from the ceiling, reading words which, when the King had first heard them two centuries before, had put him in a towering rage. They were:

"In Congress, July 4, 1776. The Unanimous Declaration of the Thirteen United States of America. When in the course of human events it becomes necessary for one people to dissolve the political bonds which have connected them with another, and to assume among the powers of the earth the separate and equal station which the laws of Nature and of Nature's God entitle them, a decent respect to the opinions of mankind requires that they should declare the causes which impel them to the separation. . . ."

The four listened in silence to the very end, to the final splendid sentence ". . . And for the support of this declaration, with a firm reliance on the protection of Divine Providence, we mutually pledge to each other our lives, our fortunes and our sacred honor."

When the President's voice ceased, Washington, Jefferson, Voltaire, and the King sat in silence for a while. It was Voltaire who first spoke.

"Magnificent," he said. "Magnificent. Also astonishing, for I understand that not a single Frenchman was consulted about drawing it up. Alas, gentlemen, we have come here on a fool's errand. We looked to find the success or failure of this interesting revolution without reflecting that it is not given to men, in their mortal lives, to succeed, but only to try to succeed.

"The problem before Man is not the manner in which he is governed. Not at all. All governments, however close to perfect, tend to corruption. No, the problem is always the spirit in which Man is governed." He turned to Jefferson. "You yourself, sir, understood that quite perfectly in your day, and summed it all up in a few words which must compel the admiration of the world to the last fading of the light of Man . . ."

"I did?" said Jefferson. "What words?"

" 'A decent respect to the opinions of mankind,' " replied Voltaire. "That is all civilization in a nutshell. For whatever the form of government, royal or republican, tyrannical or anarchic, provided that government retains constantly and actively a decent respect to the opinions of mankind, it cannot but be benevolent. All else is merely an outward show. It is always the spirit that matters. So our problem so hotly debated in Heaven, on the form of government most suitable to man proves an empty one, and there remains, for me, but one question unanswered—maybe unanswerable."

"And what is that, sir?" asked George III.

"A kind of an anguish," said Voltaire. " 'One white hand beneath the elms at Notre Dame.' "

He glanced at the angel Cecile and was charmed to see tears in her eyes.

90

Chapter Thirteen

When the President returned from reading the Declaration of Independence to the nation and the world on television, his visitors had gone. He thought for a moment that they might have decided to mingle with his other guests, and yet that would have been an odd thing to do since they were in the middle of so interesting a discussion.

They had left no note and no trace of themselves. He was perturbed because during the reading of the Declaration of Independence he had come to realize that despite the many imperfections of the American system of government, scarcely revised to meet the vast national growth and change of two hundred years, he could not advocate a return to the British system. He glanced around his office looking for his visitors to continue his discussion, and he saw in a corner an old grandfather clock which had certainly not been there before.

He reached for the telephone immediately and called Security Headquarters.

"That clock you spoke of is in my office right now," he said, a little frightened.

"Mr. President," said Storhill. "Get out of there right away. Get as far from that clock as you can. Immediately."

The President left the office and went to the far end of the corridor. Storhill rushed to him, and Tom Czeuleger went to the office and, sweating with anxiety, opened the clock case and with a pencil flashlight looked about for wires or any sign of an explosive. There were no wires and the ancient works were half gone, the few spindles and gears and rachets which remained being all covered with dust. He probed the interior with the greatest care and found nothing. He reported this to Storhill who, having searched the office thoroughly, now permitted the President to return to it.

There the President, having firmly shut the door (and having also remembered to turn off his tape recorder) requested Tom and Storhill to produce their own miniaturized recorders and put them on his desk in the "off position." When this was done he gave them a lecture.

"Something entirely remarkable has happened here in the last hour and a half which must remain a state secret for all time," he said. "I have been visited by George Washington, Thomas Jefferson, George III, and Voltaire—and a young lady whom I could not quite identify and into whose relationship with these four gentlemen I did not inquire."

"An angel," said Tom.

"Quite probably," said the President dryly. "The point is that if news of this visitation should get around, the national confidence in me would be shaken rather more than I am accustomed to. It follows that you are forbidden to make any reference to tonight's happenings at any time to anybody anywhere—and all records pertaining to those happenings are to be destroyed. Do you understand?"

"Yes," said the two.

"Any questions?"

"Sir," said Storhill, "may I suggest that if you have any records yourself, they also should be destroyed?"

"I will attend to it immediately," said the President. He turned to the tape recorder and flipped the button to "Rewind."

"Perhaps," he said as the tape hummed on the reels, "it would do no harm to listen just once to the slightly disturbing conversation I had with my visitors. It was very instructive. You may listen as witnesses. Then I will burn the tape."

When the tape was rewound the President pressed the "Play" button. For a while there was only the hiss of the power flow and then came the words, in a beautifully modulated voice . . . "a decent respect to the opinions of mankind . . . a decent respect to the opinions of mankind . . . a decent respect to the opinions of mankind." There was nothing else.

"I can't understand it," said the President. "This thing isn't working properly." He tried turning it on again, but all he got over and over again was the same sentence. "A decent respect to the opinions of mankind . . ."

"Mr. President," said Tom, "I think there may be a kind of a hex on White House tape recorders. But may I respectfully suggest that you do not destroy this particular tape, but order that it be passed on from President to President, to be played regularly by whoever should occupy the White House in the years to come?"

The President gave him a hard, penetrating look, and said, "An excellent suggestion."

At that moment the door of the office opened, and two rather plump ladies in panniered dresses entered, accompanied by a gray-haired porter with a number of campaign ribbons on the breast of his jacket. He seemed to be in charge of them.

"There," he said, beckoning to the clock, "no need to panic. Management never overlooks anything." He opened the front of the clock and the two ladies, greatly relieved, and with the merest bob to the others present, entered. The porter followed, but before pulling the door closed he said to the President in an inquiring tone, "I expect you got the message, sir?" And then, with a general glance about, he added, "See you all again—I hope."

It was Storhill who first recovered and streaked to the

front of the clock and opened it. He found it empty and turned away stunned. "I can't understand it," he said. "I can't understand it."

"Don't try," said the President. "That is often the wisest course in such circumstances."

Back in Heaven Voltaire set out on his morning stroll through the Elysian fields. They were as lovely as ever—miles and miles of iris in purple and pale blue, in gold and pink and white, stately groves of ash and elm with white unicorns standing gracefully in the shade, and here and there a jeweled wyvern, basking in the sun.

There were angels and archangels, cherubs, and seraphs, thrones, principalities and powers and saints of every degree, all enchantingly happy, all that is except Voltaire, who was just a little bit ruffled. So, ignoring the delights about, he marched straight through the lilies and the joyful throng to The Club and there he tackled the porter.

"My friend," he said, "I am beginning to suspect that I am only a tool in the hands of the management—that all that happened recently (you know precisely what I mean) was planned or programmed, as they put it now, and that I had no voluntary part in it. This, if true, makes a mockery of free will. What have you to say about that?"

A wyvern, who had just leaped into the sky in an excess of joy to cry, "Gloria in excelsis Deo," overheard this and fell back to earth wordless.

But the archangel Gabriel was not put out. "Saint Voltaire," he said, "I am not very bright, I just do my job and I'm happy doing it. But if you think your adventure on Earth, which started with a somewhat improbable meeting between Queen Charlotte and Saint Martha Washington, was programmed and you object to that, then it must occur to you that your present attitude may also be programmed and what you call your free will, programmed as well. So why don't you just settle down and enjoy yourself?"

"Gabriel," cried Voltaire, "you have just set my mind in a turmoil."

"I am very glad to hear it," said the archangel, "for I know that you love a turmoil. Now if you will excuse me I have the chairs to set out for the lawn bowling this afternoon."

He watched Voltaire's retreating figure, but instead of getting busy with the chairs, he went instead to the armory and looked over the racks of spears against the walls and the great flaming swords, the shining bucklers and the gleaming bows and quivers of arrows. He glanced at his campaign ribbons and recalled Lucifer's great revolt in Heaven, which had started with complaints about programming or something of the sort.

He sighed. He was an old soldier and he certainly wouldn't question the wisdom of the High Command. But left to him there would not have been any Earth, and there wouldn't have been any Tree of Knowledge in the Garden of Eden if there *had* been an Earth.

Then, obedient as always, he started putting out the chairs.

A few days later on Earth when the people of the United States each in their varying time zones turned on the Six O'Clock News (a ritual which had replaced family prayer in many sections of the country) they were greeted by a picture of George III having his feet sprayed and holding aloft a can and saying "Simpkins Soothing Spray—there's a kingdom of comfort in it." The effect on the whole was good. The King seemed a nice, kind, honest, comforting kind of man—just the sort who would make for a good President should he care to run for office.

But the British Ambassador in Washington objected to

the commercial, for he was a man of little foresight, and the film strip was withdrawn a few days later in favor of a famous black basketball player doing the same thing, the wording being changed to "Simpkins Soothing Footspray—Scores with a rebound."

As for Lieutenant Tom Czeuleger, on the President's orders it was thought better to let him remain on White House duty with the detachment of Marines who guard the White House. He therefore had many occasions to see Jennie and for a while they did not discuss the remarkable events which had occurred at the Bicentennial Ball.

Tom, having a tidy mind, tried to bring the matter up once or twice, but Jennie cut him off. The last time he approached the matter Jennie turned on him, and with her mouth set as hard as Vermont granite said, "That whole evening was make-believe and that whole happening was a dream."

"Well, when two people share a common dream," said Tom, "it seems to me that that's the strongest possible sign that they should share their dreams for the rest of their lives."

"I was wondering when you were going to ask me," said Jennie. And so they were married and lived happily ever afterward.